SIN AND THE SOLDIER

Gentlemen of Pleasure, Book 3

Mary Lancaster

ARE YOU SIGNED UP FOR DRAGONBLADE'S BLOG?

You'll get the latest news and information on exclusive giveaways, exclusive excerpts, coming releases, sales, free books, cover reveals and more.

Check out our complete list of authors, too!

No spam, no junk. That's a promise!

Sign Up Here

www.dragonbladepublishing.com

Dearest Reader;

Thank you for your support of a small press. At Dragonblade Publishing, we strive to bring you the highest quality Historical Romance from some of the best authors in the business. Without your support, there is no 'us', so we sincerely hope you adore these stories and find some new favorite authors along the way.

Happy Reading!

CEO, Dragonblade Publishing

Additional Dragonblade books by Author Mary Lancaster

Gentlemen of Pleasure
The Devil and the Viscount (Book 1)
Temptation and the Artist (Book 2)
Sin and the Soldier (Book 3)
Debauchery and the Earl (Book 4)

Pleasure Garden Series
Unmasking the Hero (Book 1)
Unmasking Deception (Book 2)
Unmasking Sin (Book 3)
Unmasking the Duke (Book 4)
Unmasking the Thief (Book 5)

Crime & Passion Series
Mysterious Lover
Letters to a Lover
Dangerous Lover

The Husband Dilemma Series
How to Fool a Duke

Season of Scandal Series
Pursued by the Rake
Abandoned to the Prodigal
Married to the Rogue
Unmasked by her Lover
Her Star from the East (Novella)

Imperial Season Series
Vienna Waltz
Vienna Woods
Vienna Dawn

Blackhaven Brides Series
The Wicked Baron
The Wicked Lady
The Wicked Rebel
The Wicked Husband
The Wicked Marquis
The Wicked Governess
The Wicked Spy
The Wicked Gypsy
The Wicked Wife
Wicked Christmas (A Novella)
The Wicked Waif
The Wicked Heir
The Wicked Captain
The Wicked Sister

Unmarriageable Series
The Deserted Heart
The Sinister Heart
The Vulgar Heart
The Broken Heart
The Weary Heart
The Secret Heart
Christmas Heart

The Lyon's Den Connected World
Fed to the Lyon

De Wolfe Pack: The Series
The Wicked Wolfe
Vienna Wolfe

Also from Mary Lancaster
Madeleine

CHAPTER ONE

WHEN THE APPLAUSE erupted, Captain Lord Richard Gorse rose to his feet with everyone else.

Not because the harpist had astonished him with the power and flawless delight of her playing—he had listened to her far too often for these things to surprise him—but because tonight, he actually intended to speak to her. And with one arm and a game leg, he needed a head start on the rest of the crowd. It wasn't as if he could actually clap to show his appreciation.

The harpist, whose name he didn't know—it hadn't even been on the handbills advertising this rare evening concert at Renwick's Hotel—rose from her chair and curtseyed gracefully. She smiled, transforming her face from fine, almost severe beauty, to dazzling loveliness, and her gaze rested on Richard as it sometimes did. Occasionally, he allowed himself to imagine that it gave her courage or even pleasure to see his familiar figure among her audience. More likely, she was wary of the constant presence of a stranger and regarded him as a potential threat.

He might have imagined her faint nod of recognition before her gaze passed on. But he did *not* imagine the way she froze a moment later. For a tiny instant, her eyes were fixed and steady, appalled to the point of downright fear. And then they moved on, her smile reanimated.

Richard turned with inappropriate wrath to see who had

caused her discomfort. Of course, he could not tell for sure, but the back of a male head was darting among the audience as though escaping. Perhaps he had been as disconcerted as the harpist. No doubt there was a tale to tell. A tale that didn't include Richard and never would.

But he could, at least, do her some good in return for the help she had so unconsciously given him. So, he stayed no longer to worship at the harpist's feet, but limped off at speed down the aisle, the tapping of his cane inaudible in the continuing roar of appreciation.

Like all decent soldiers, Richard had reconnoitered the terrain and knew the only way out of the room behind the stage.

HE HAD FOUND her.

Natalie knew she should never have agreed to this series of evening concerts at the hotel.

The afternoon concerts in the pleasure gardens were one thing, much more muted in terms of publicity. As it was, the only way she would agree to play in the hotel of an evening was if her name was kept out of it. Bill Renwick and the hotel manager had both pleaded with her, but she had been adamant, and in the end, the advertising bills had declaimed only, *An evening with our delightful harpist and orchestra.*

And everything had felt soothingly familiar. She played the same instrument, accompanied in various pieces by the orchestra she was used to. The injured soldier with the haunted face sat in the front row, to her left. She had received a welcome reception on her entrance and rapturous applause at her bow.

It had been a relief. Her only regret had been that the soldier did not appear as soothed as normal by her playing, but then she had only allowed herself a brief glance at him before her gaze had moved on. And that was when she had seen Gerald.

How? How had he found her after more than two years, in the middle of nowhere?

Well, Renwick's Hotel was not *nowhere*. It was on the edges of London, though, nowhere near the fashionable or theatrical quarters. It stood on the grounds of Maida Pleasure Gardens, which were more known for vulgar entertainments than refined arts. And yet, there Gerald was in the audience. He did not even look surprised, damn his soul. He just smiled, as though pleased with her performance.

What a pity it would be her last. She had grown comfortable here, made a life and a modest living around her music. She had made friends among the orchestra and the garden staff. Even Bill Renwick himself, the owner of the gardens and the hotel, had become *almost* a friend. Certainly, he had felt like security, protection.

Well, no longer.

Somehow, she got off the stage. She knew she should linger, to congratulate the orchestra, to discuss the performance with them as usual, over a cup of tea or a glass of wine, if Renwick was feeling generous. But she had one aim—to get to her cottage before Gerald could follow her.

He might have found the cottage already. Nausea almost overwhelmed her. She all but bolted across the room toward the door. And then it opened, and Gerald walked in.

He closed it behind him, smiling.

"Natalie," he said fondly. "At last."

She stilled, like a deer before it bolts, only she had nowhere to bolt to. No covering forest. Except, behind her came the hum and shuffle of the orchestra exiting the stage.

"Beautifully played, Miss Nat!" Arthur, the first violinist called cheerfully. "Very fine indeed."

"Thank you," she replied into the buzz of agreement. She turned toward them with relief. They could be her shield, even if just for a few moments. "I am happy to return the compliment, gentlemen. Especially in the last movement, the music soared."

The compliments descended inevitably into more technical discussion, where Natalie was happy to wallow indefinitely. From the corner of her eye, though, she saw that Gerald was not deterred. Indeed, leaning one shoulder against the wall, he looked both amused and as patient as a spider in the center of its web, while the talk went on and the musicians put away their instruments.

And then, Gerald's voice said behind her. "Perhaps you would join me in a glass of wine, Natalie?"

Her flesh crawled with as much fear as hatred. But at least the fear made her angry. She did not have to speak to him. She certainly did not have to drink with him.

She cast him a look of contempt that she hoped cut him. "That is not possible."

"You have a previous engagement, perhaps?" Gerald mocked.

She lifted her chin. "I do."

"I shall not keep you long from your…engagement," Gerald said. "But we need a brief discussion."

"No," she said tightly. She was damned if she would make it easy for him. "We have had our last discussion. If you will excuse me—"

"I'm afraid I must insist," Gerald said with just that playful tone she most hated covering the implacable instruction that still made her want to cringe or flee or both.

"*I'm* afraid you left your manners elsewhere," said a voice she had never heard before. Deep, clipped, unignorable. "The lady has spoken."

Almost bemused by the offer of rescue, impossible as it would inevitably be, she turned her head and beheld the injured soldier. There was nothing haunted about his scarred yet handsome face now. It merely commanded. He may not have been in uniform, but he was every inch the officer whom no soldier would dare to disobey, overlaid, perhaps, with the supercilious aristocrat.

"She has spoken, yes, but not to you, sir," Gerald pointed out, still amused.

The soldier's expression never wavered. He merely transferred his wintry gaze to her and bowed. "May I escort you, ma'am?"

The choice, it seemed, was still the same. Compliance or defiance, and she had long since decided on the latter, whatever trouble it brought in its wake. And the trouble would be hers, not the soldier's.

"Thank you, sir," she said clearly, and, leaving space between them for him to maneuver his walking stick, she laid her hand lightly on his sleeve.

As he turned, he flicked a look in the direction of the orchestra members. That, too, looked like a command, and as she and the soldier began to walk to the door, several musicians fell in behind them.

"Are you a musician, too?" the first violinist asked, apparently addressing Gerald.

"How is it you know our Miss Natalie?" asked another.

"I have to leave here," she said intensely to the soldier. "And he must not see me."

"Then trust me." He left her to close the door, and turned sharp left, away from the front door, though there was another at the back of the foyer into the gardens.

Bill Renwick was strolling to intercept them, one of his sons at his side bearing a tray of champagne and glasses. *Oh, the devil! Now he chooses such generosity?*

"For the orchestra," the soldier said to Bill in the same, clipped, quiet tones. "The lady will join you later, when you have discreetly ejected your uninvited guest."

Bill's gaze flew to hers in both astonishment and dismay. She nodded once and swept onward on the arm of the soldier, whose pace was surprisingly rapid considering its unevenness. He pushed open a door with his shoulder, and she found herself on a clean, narrow staircase, no doubt one for staff use. Although somewhat gloomy, it was lit to some degree from wall sconces, so it was only when they emerged, at last, into a more brightly lit passage that she thought to wonder where on earth he was taking her.

These were the rooms where well-to-do guests stayed, usually for a mere night or two to break their journey or to take care of business in town, although, according to rumor, the rooms were also taken for less moral purposes. Some gentlemen entertained their mistresses here.

She dropped his arm in sudden, almost baffled suspicion. Had she jumped from the frying pan into the proverbial fire? He found a key in his coat pocket and slid it into the lock of the nearest door, which he opened to reveal what looked like a sitting room and stood aside for her to enter.

Now, belatedly, she stepped back, ready to bolt.

"I'm no threat to you, ma'am," he said impatiently. "Take your chances elsewhere by all means, but you seemed to need a little extra help."

She stared into his hard, wintry blue eyes which seemed to be merely a reflection of his abrupt and testy voice. She took a deep breath and brushed past him into the room.

It was quite an elegant, comfortable apartment. The red and gold military coat she had seen him wear often before, hung carelessly over the back of a chair. A book lay on the sofa. In the wall opposite, another closed door led, presumably, to his bedchamber.

"Please, sit." He had followed her in, spun, and turned the key in the lock with one surprisingly deft movement before he limped past her further into the room. That he left the key in the lock was some comfort to her. She took a few paces and sat on the edge of the sofa.

Her host tossed his walking stick onto the armchair at right angles to the sofa, then moved to a cabinet where he lifted a decanter and poured two measures of what looked like brandy. Carrying them both in his one hand, he placed them on the table before the sofa and pushed one toward her.

"For medicinal purposes," he murmured, and moving the

stick to the floor, propped up against the chair arm, he sat. "It's not quite champagne, but you seem to have had a shock."

"I have," she admitted, snatching up the glass. "And I thank you for your help." She took a sizeable gulp of brandy, which snatched at her breath but at least shocked her brain back into clear thought. "I have to go home without him seeing." Her eyes flew to the soldier's. "What if he knows where I live already? He could have taken everything. Again."

"Then you have recourse to a magistrate. Not to mention Bill Renwick. I understand he takes a dim view of anyone else thieving on the premises. Who is this man who has cut up your peace?"

A small sound broke from her, as much sob as laughter. "That's exactly what he has done. A hard-fought peace. Like yours, I imagine."

He looked unexpectedly rattled by that, taking a hasty drink from his glass.

"His name is Gerald Monck," she said. "And I am engaged to marry him."

He paused and then leaned forward to set his glass back down on the table. For a long moment, he did not look at her, then slowly, he lifted his gaze to her face. "You'll forgive me for remarking that you do not appear to be a willing bride."

"I am not."

"Then you shall not marry him."

She could not help smiling at that. "You sound so sure, I could almost believe you."

"The law requires agreement from both parties."

"You are a soldier, are you not? An officer?"

He blinked. "Sort of."

Sort of? "You are used to fighting by certain rules, by a code of honor. Gerald is not. One never knows how low he will go until he gets there."

"My dear lady, we can all fight dirty. If I am to help you, I suspect your confidence will be necessary. For now, what is the most important thing I can do for you?"

He asked so simply, so casually, that she was taken unawares. It almost seemed natural to rely on him, a stranger with whom she had never even spoken before tonight. A troubled, haunted man who turned up frequently to her afternoon recitals in the pleasure garden.

She could not even remember when she had first noticed him there—more than a year ago, perhaps nearer two. In recent months, he had always sat in the same place, at the left-hand end of the front row, no doubt for ease of escape. But she had noticed him before then, the one-armed cavalry officer whose face betrayed pain and suffering way beyond her own, and yet who watched and listened with such intensity it almost disconcerted her. Until she had noticed that as she played, the lines of his suffering seemed to ease. His eyes seemed less haunted when she had finished. In some, insubstantial, unmeasurable way, he had given her purpose and confidence, and she had taken her own comfort in whatever she had managed to give him. And if the odd romantic fantasy crept into her mind—well, a girl could dream. It was, by far, the safest form of romance.

It had been a strange, silent intimacy that she might well have imagined. And now he asked, *"What is the most important thing I can do for you?"*

"He will steal my music," she blurted. "I need to get it and hide it."

"Where is it?"

He didn't even ask what sort of music or why it was important. Her heart warmed. Perhaps it was the brandy.

"You are very kind," she said with difficulty. "I have not even thanked you. In truth, you have already done the most vital thing possible by hiding me for now. The staff here will be able to help me escape unseen, even if he is staying at the hotel." And if he could afford the prices at the hotel then he was doing well for himself, so why should he bother with her?

"There are cheaper rooms in the other wing," the soldier

observed as if he read her thoughts.

She met his gaze. "I don't even know your name," she blurted.

"Richard Gorse." He sounded distracted, his thoughts elsewhere.

"Captain?" she guessed.

He shrugged, a sardonic smile twisting his long, expressive lips. "Sort of. I haven't sold out. I'm still on half-pay, though I can't imagine what use I'd be. And you? Your… betrothed called you Natalie."

"Natalie Derwent."

"You kept your name private, unadvertised in order to avoid your betrothed?"

"Don't call him that," she said quickly, and entirely unreasonably, but he didn't quarrel, let alone point out that it was she who had said they were engaged. She took one last sip of her brandy for strength and set it back down on the table with determination. "Thank you for rescuing me, Captain. I shall be safe to slip away now."

He rose when she did, using the stick to lever himself up as she had seen him do so many times before.

He was frowning. "I would be happier escorting you to wherever it is you live."

The habit of secrecy had become so ingrained that she hesitated. But Gerald had been the reason for her secrecy, and he had already found her. The soldier—Captain Gorse—had already proved he was her ally.

"I live in a cottage outside the gardens," she said, "but I would not give you the trouble of walking so far."

"It will be less trouble than the alternative," he murmured. "Have you no wrap against the evening chill?"

When was the last time anyone had worried about her being cold? Almost three years ago, before her mother died. After two and a half years of fierce independence, it felt curiously sweet to be cared for, even in such a mundane matter.

"I left a cloak at the desk downstairs," she said.

"Come, then. We'll use the staff stairs again for discretion."

This time, he preceded her down the stairs and did not offer his arm, leaving it free, perhaps, to make use of his stick.

The foyer was quiet, save for a family who had clearly just arrived, their trunks still being unloaded from the carriage on the front drive.

"I'll be but a moment," Natalie murmured and hurried up to the reception desk, where she helped herself to her folded cloak from the shelf beside the distracted clerk. When she turned back, Captain Gorse remained where she had left him, though he had clearly been scanning the hall and the staircase for Gerald.

They left by the back door, through the formal hotel garden. If she didn't walk through the pleasure gardens on the other side, she usually took a shortcut over the meadow. In consideration of the captain's lame leg, to say nothing of her own best "performance" gown, she led him to the road, and they walked up the hill.

"Does your leg pain you?" she asked abruptly.

"When it rains. Less when I exercise it more."

She smiled in the darkness. "Then I am doing you a favor?"

"Exactly."

They walked in silence for a little, and she was reminded that when she had seen him among the audience tonight, in his usual place, her nerves had quieted, and she played well. Very well, she suspected, for it had been one of those moving, only-the-music experiences that happened only rarely for her. She had been elated. Until she had seen Gerald there, smiling like Lucifer come upon a new temptation.

"Where did you study music?" he asked.

She smiled. "Everywhere. I had an excellent governess, and a neighbor's tutor helped me further. I traveled a little in the west of Scotland and Ireland and Wales, learning more about the harp and traditional harp music. And I had some training in an unofficial way from maestros in Paris and Vienna."

"You traveled alone?" he asked with more curiosity than judgment.

"No, usually with my mother or my governess. Both of them after my brother died and we went to Paris in 1814, when the war ended. We managed to flee to Vienna when Bonaparte came back, and then went south to Italy. We met Gerald in Italy. Probably around the time you were fighting the Battle of Waterloo… Were you at Waterloo?"

"It's where I lost my arm. What happened to your mother? And the governess?"

"Gerald persuaded my mother to dismiss Amelia—Miss Dart—which I didn't discover until we had left her far behind. I was ill at the time. She must have thought I—we—had abandoned her. I suppose we did. I never found out what happened to her."

"And your mother?"

Natalie swallowed. "She died. Some fever, perhaps bad water. I was filling quite large concert halls by then." Perhaps she hadn't kept the bitterness from her voice, for he glanced at her as if he could see her expression in the pale, erratic lantern light. She couldn't make out his, although the scar down one side of his face seemed to shine. "The cottage is just a few hundred yards down this track. You don't have to—"

"Lay on, Macduff," he interrupted with flippancy, and indeed the track seemed to give him little more trouble than the road. She worried about him walking back alone.

There was no light in her cottage. She thought that was a good sign.

"Do you live alone?" he asked. "No maid?"

"No."

"Then, if you please, I will go in first and make sure everything is secure."

Her stomach twisted in alarm at his words, and yet they were only sensible. It was only later, when he had unlocked the door, lit the candle, and walked round the tiny dwelling, that she wondered how much good a lame, one-armed soldier would be against Gerald or however many ruffians he might hire to intimidate her or steal from her.

CHAPTER TWO

S HE WAS UNEASY about him being in her house. He couldn't tell if she hated the invasion of her privacy, was ashamed of the tiny, basic dwelling, or feared he would be hard to get rid of again. Thrusting her anxieties to the back of his mind, he concentrated on making sure she was as safe as she could be.

There was no one skulking in the cottage, and her three windows were all closed and locked. Only when he had assured himself of this did he allow himself to see more, as he lit several candles, with which she seemed to be liberally supplied. The cottage, he suspected had once been a single room. But partition walls had been installed to make a small bedchamber and a tiny kitchen. Everything was neat and clean, except the dining table which was covered with pages and pages of musical notation, with pen and inkstand half-covered. A small square pianoforte sat open under the window, a hard chair in front of the keyboard. By the empty fireplace was a single, worn but well-upholstered armchair.

A chipped vase containing a mix of bright, colorful flowers adorned the windowsill, but that seemed to be the only ornamentation in the sitting room. Without warning, he ached for her, for her loneliness.

She was gathering up pages from the table, sorting them into a neat pile. These were what she feared Gerald Monck would take from her?

"Would you like a cup of tea before you face the walk back?" she asked, perhaps to make sure he knew she expected him to leave.

"No, thank you. I don't care for the stuff, to be honest."

"At least sit," she offered, indicating the armchair as she brushed past him with her handful of music. She took it into the bedchamber, and he saw her placing it in a chest of drawers, adding it to other piles of paper.

Propping his cane against the table, he picked up the wooden chair and placed it opposite the armchair, before fetching the walking stick and sitting. He probably didn't need the cane anymore to aid his rise from a chair, but too many undignified moments made him reluctant to risk it in front of her.

"You came to speak to me," she said in a rush, walking back into the sitting room and closing the door.

"I did?"

"After the concert, you came to find me. You've never done that before."

He wondered if he was actually blushing and laughed at himself, which at least enabled him to carry the moment with a touch of sardonic humor. "True, but then I have had little enough to say before except what you already know."

"What I already know?" she repeated, confused. She glanced at the armchair, where she had clearly expected him to sit, then sat in it herself, her movements as quick and graceful as on the stage.

"That I enjoy your playing. You knew it already and must hear it from everyone all the time, so there seemed little point in disturbing you with mundanities."

She blinked, a smile flickering across her face. "You have an odd idea of mundanities. I assure you that musicians never tire of praise. Be that as it may, am I to understand you had something else to say to me?"

As if suddenly realizing what that something might be, she

tensed. Her fingers grasped each other hard in her lap and in the soft glow of the candlelight, he saw the pink tinge to her skin. She was a kind young woman. It would hurt her to turn him down. Had he ever intended to make the request she so clearly feared?

He said, "My sister-in-law is planning to entertain a few friends in the autumn. It would not be a large gathering by town standards, but she would like to provide something a little different for her guests in terms of music. I told her I would ask you to call upon her."

Her eyebrows flew up in astonishment.

"It will be a smaller audience than tonight's," he said, "but those present could be a significant help to your career."

For a moment, an excitement that was almost hunger flared in her eyes, and then she tore her gaze free. "How kind you were to think of me, to recommend me. Thank you! But I…I cannot stay here any longer."

"You will let this Monck drive you away?"

She nodded tiredly. "There is no alternative."

"There is," he snapped. He probably sounded angry, for her gaze flew back to his.

"You don't understand. He has no scruples, no…honor. He will take everything, compel me—" She broke off with an impatient gesture of one hand. "It doesn't matter. I won't give him anything, but that means I cannot stay here."

He searched her face. "No one should be compelled. And you must know you have friends to protect you. Your fellow musicians jumped to help instantly. So did Bill Renwick, and he is not a negligible ally. Neither am I, surprisingly enough."

The intense focus that she brought to her harp seemed now to be on him. Curious, wary, baffled, and yet, surely, with a hint of something very like hope. Her eyes were beautiful in the candlelight, soft yet gleaming with intelligence. "You think me a poor creature," she said sadly.

"No."

"You don't know me at all," she said with a spurt of impatience.

"No. But I would like to."

Not fear, but challenge glared at him now. "Why?"

Now, he wished he wasn't looking at her. He could stand up and walk away and keep his privacy intact. Or he could try for the connection he secretly wanted.

"Because I am a troubled man and you have brought me a modicum of peace." His lips twisted. "So, you see, there is a debt."

He rose before she could deny it or pity him. The peace she brought had never been about pity, and he was damned if he would allow it to be contaminated now.

"You're wrong," she said unexpectedly. "Of course, there is no debt. I play and the audience listens, takes from the music what they will. That has always been the unwritten contract between musician and audience."

"I will not argue debts with you, Miss Derwent. It is far too late to argue anything at all. But think about what I have said. You cannot want to be running all your life. Retreating. Sometimes, when you have the necessary troops and defenses, you have to stand."

"Are you standing?" she retorted.

He raised his arm, walking stick in the air. "Just."

She smiled, directly at him, not at some amorphous, applauding audience. And in that delicious, gut-wrenching moment, he would have died for her.

WHEN HE RETURNED to the hotel, Richard was not entirely surprised to find Bill Renwick approaching him across the dim foyer.

"Can your lordship spare me a moment?" Renwick inquired.

"Several," Richard said at once. "I was hoping to speak to

you."

"This way." Renwick led him through an office behind the reception desk and then through a semi-hidden door, which he closed as soon as they were both inside.

It was a small office, with little more than a desk, two hard chairs, and a tall cabinet, but it was sensibly lit, even at this hour, and there was a carpet on the floor.

"Natalie Derwent," Renwick said without preamble, "is not without friends."

"Good. Because I think she will need them. Do you know that miscreant who approached her after the concert?"

Renwick blinked. "No. That is, he does seem familiar but I'm damned if I know why. However, my main concern with your lordship is to ensure Miss Derwent doesn't fall from the frying pan into the fire. If you catch my meaning."

"Perfectly. And it is not my intention to harm Miss Derwent. On the contrary, I admire her talent and would like to see it better known."

"Would you?"

"It's Gerald Monck who is the threat to her," Richard said bluntly. "Is he staying at the hotel?"

"No. He came by hackney and left the same way. Asked to be dropped in Piccadilly."

Richard's lips twitched. "I knew you were an observant man. She's afraid of him. Thinks he'll spoil things for her here. Steal from her."

"Not under my nose," Renwick said with a hint of heartening grimness. "Did you leave her at the cottage?"

"Unharmed," Richard drawled. "When do you expect her tomorrow?"

"Around midday. There is a concert in the rose garden."

"She does not come earlier?"

"Not usually. She works in her cottage."

"And walks to the gardens? Alone?"

"As a rule."

Richard stirred. "I would escort the lady, but I fear for her reputation should she be seen too much in my company."

"And should she send you away with a flea in your ear," Renwick mocked.

"That, too."

"One of my sons will bring her in the pony and trap. He has things to collect from the farm first."

Richard nodded. "Are you her landlord?"

"No. I offered her lodging, like most of my people, but she's wary of her employer controlling the roof over her head. She's wary of a lot of things."

"I would put that largely down to Monck."

"I'll find out what I can," Renwick promised.

"So will I. I have a friend who specializes in such matters."

Renwick regarded him uneasily. "Not Mr. Dunne?"

Richard smiled.

Renwick groaned. "Gorse. Of course. You're related to that cove who got off the murder charge."

"My little brother."

"God save us."

Richard leaned on his cane and rose to his feet. "We might at least hope for the Almighty's benevolent indifference. I'll bid you good night, Mr. Renwick."

"You're only staying the one night," Renwick remarked as he opened the door.

"Are the rooms bespoken elsewhere?"

"Not yet."

"Then I shall stay on for a day or so. If you have no objection?"

"None *yet*," Renwick said, and they parted in perfect understanding.

NATALIE WOKE WITH several things clear in her head.

If she was going to stand and fight, she needed Captain Gorse to help her plan the campaign. And she would need the support of Bill Renwick and his staff.

The question was, could she risk them? Gerald was pitiless, but she doubted he would risk hurting anyone but her. Bill was only just on the right side of the law—mostly—but his reach was long, by all accounts, and only a fool would make an enemy of him. Gerald had never been a fool.

Captain Gorse, on the other hand, was wounded in mind and body. She had always known that, even before he had said a word to her. And yet there was a relentless, steely strength in him, too. He never gave up. Even when he had left last night, he had said, "Think about my sister-in-law's proposal. I am happy to escort you to her whenever you wish."

Well, maybe that would be possible, too. She had no reason to hide when Gerald had already found her. Of course, it would be one more fee for him to take away from her if he could.

If he could.

She rose, washed, and dressed before, with something like dread, she drew back the curtains. She half expected Gerald to be camped outside or peering in. But she saw no one. Forcing herself, she went about her morning routine, making tea, toasting some of yesterday's bread, which she slathered with butter and enjoyed while sitting on the front step in the morning sunshine.

Then she went back inside, took care of a little necessary laundry, and sat down at the pianoforte. She was working on the final movement of her symphony. It had been filling her head for days, but now the music would not come. The melody she had been so pleased with sounded trite and vulgar and kept slipping into something else that did not fit the piece. In desperation, she ignored the pianoforte and turned to the harp. Here, in triumph, she found the way to make her melody flow and argue with the piano. If she could get her friend Laurie to play the piano part for her, she could find how to make it work.

She scribbled down the basic notation before she lost it again, then returned to the harp and found the new music occupying her head instead, low, insistent, building to…something. Something, special, something beyond good.

Damn, why can I never stick to one task? Dragging a fresh sheet of music, she hastily jotted down the new notes. And became aware of the rumbling of wheels on the track past the cottage.

In sudden panic, she jumped to her feet and bolted the door. She consulted her father's old pocket watch and realized she should be changing for the noon concert. But she could not leave her place at the window until whoever was out there had passed.

It was a pony and provision-laden cart, driven by young Rob Renwick. He must have come from the Fenners' farm. The pony stopped, and Rob waved to her. In relief, she went out to speak to him.

If he noticed the unbolting of the front door, he said nothing.

"Can I take you up to the gardens?" he offered cheerfully.

It was so much her habit to say no, that she almost did. But Captain Gorse had been right. She needed her troops. "If you don't mind waiting five minutes while I change and fetch some things?"

"No hurry for me."

She changed quickly into her decent morning gown, which was the most comfortable for playing the harp in daytime and in changeable weather. Then, greatly daring, she took out her carpet bag and loaded it with the symphony music she had completed so far. After a moment's hesitation, she left what she had been working on over the last couple of days, sure she could remember it well enough. The important thing was to be sure Gerald never laid his hands on anything he could use or sell.

Ron blinked when he saw the carpet bag. "Not leaving us are you, Miss Nat?"

"Hardly." She placed the bag in the cart and climbed up beside him. She imagined unseen eyes watching her, guessing what was in the bag, following the slow progress of the cart toward the road. And she hated how frayed her nerves had become.

Damn Gerald. Damn him all over again.

Although the back of her neck prickled for the first part of the journey, she forced herself not to keep glancing back over her shoulder.

"Are you stopping at the hotel?" she asked. "I believe I will go there first."

"Right you are, Miss Nat."

He drew up eventually outside the kitchens. Even though the cart was quickly swarmed with people fetching much-needed supplies for the hotel and the tearoom, Rob Renwick helped Natalie down and retrieved her bag with a quick smile before seeing to the unloading of the cart.

For a moment, alone in the swarm of business, Natalie hesitated.

What if Captain Gorse had left the hotel? Gone home with the realization that her ridiculous problems were not his?

Then I shall make alternative plans. Determinedly, she walked through the kitchen door. She would not risk an encounter with Gerald in the foyer, not when she carried the precious cargo in her bag. Instead, she used the staff stairs and emerged opposite the captain's room with butterflies in her stomach, even though the passage was empty of all save the maids chattering as they cleaned farther along.

Taking a deep breath, she marched up to his door and knocked briskly.

To her relief, there was immediate stirring inside, the scraping of a chair on the floor. She stood back, her heart hammering, and the door swung open.

Captain Gorse stood there in his shirt and pantaloons, his hair tousled. For no reason, Natalie flushed from her toes. She had no idea why, except that she had never seen him less than neatly, impeccably turned out, whether in uniform or civilian dress, even the last time she had entered this room. There was a new intimacy in seeing him like this, his hair uncombed, the strong column of his throat rising from the open neck of his shirt, his empty sleeve dangling.

His eyes, blue, wintry, impatient, changed at once, though there was no time to read his expression. He glanced quickly up and down the passage to make sure she was not observed, and then stood back for her to enter.

"Miss Derwent," he said.

She brushed past him into the room and heard the door close. "I am sorry to disturb you. But I wanted to ask a favor of you before the concert begins. There is no problem if you would rather not. I have other possibilities. But—"

From behind her, his fingers closed around the handles of her bag, and despite the fact that she had been about to give it to him, she resisted, swinging around to face him. He stood too tall and too close, though his fingers at once released the bag.

He straightened, though he did not step back. "I meant only to lay it down for you, so that you might sit."

"Sorry." She wished he did not loom over her, and yet he smelled deliciously of warm, clean male, of some spice and lime soap that…intrigued. She dropped the bag at her feet and inhaled his scent before she said, "My fingers seem reluctant to part with it, though I came here to ask you to look after it for me."

"Of course."

She couldn't help her quick smile. "Just *of course?* Not *what is in it?* No, *how long do you expect me to keep it?* Or *how much trouble will it bring me?*"

His lips might have stretched a little in response, but it was hard to tell when his steady, unblinking gaze held hers captive. His focus flickered downward, to her mouth, and butterflies swished in her stomach.

And *then* he stepped back. "Perhaps you'll sit and explain it to me."

CHAPTER THREE

GERALD MONCK WAS indebted to a pretty little songbird called Amy Laurel for the information that Natalie lived in a cottage across the path from the pleasure gardens.

"Alone?" he asked, steering her off the main path where a man he was sure he recognized from the previous evening was hurrying in their direction.

"Quite alone," Amy said, as though amused. "Very respectable is our Miss Nat."

"Is she?" Monck asked, allowing surprise into his voice. "And yet there was some man hanging around her last night. Tall fellow with one arm."

"Oh *him*. He doesn't even speak to her, just comes for the music. Captain, he is, injured in the war. And a lord. Lord Richard Gorse, to be precise."

"Sounds as if you know him pretty well," Monck teased, storing away the name to run past his more respectable new acquaintances in town.

She blushed. "Well, I wouldn't mind. Even with an arm missing and that scar down his face, there's something about him... And he's a thorough gentleman. I tried to flirt with him once, but he didn't even notice me. He doesn't notice anyone but Natalie."

"Really? When to most of us, you are younger and prettier." He smiled alluringly, which made her blush even harder.

"Sir, I have to go. I'm singing at the midday concert, and I have to be there for the start. Come and hear me if you like. Natalie plays before me."

Does she, by God? "Perhaps I will."

As the girl skipped off, Monck went in search of his recently acquired henchman, who went by the name of Dan. He found him propped against a tree, gazing rather longingly toward the tables where tea, food, and ices were being served. When Monck gestured peremptorily, the man pushed himself upright with obvious reluctance and sauntered toward him.

"Don't rush on my account," Monck said sarcastically.

"It's a pleasure garden," Dan retorted. "You start quick marching about the place, people ask themselves why. But if you've got the answers—"

"Never mind that," Monck interrupted. "She lives in a cottage just beyond the pleasure garden. *That* direction, I would guess from where my informant looked when she told me."

Dan considered. "There's a gate up there and a path of sorts that leads to a couple of cottages. Could be one of them."

"Then let us go and see," Monck said, "and you can show off your burglary skills."

"Mind your gab," Dan muttered.

NATALIE SAT ON the sofa in Richard's sitting room and watched him limp to the desk, where he seemed to have been working, and pull a coat from the back of the chair. He flung the coat about his shoulders, then wrestled his one arm into the sleeve. It was a maneuver that must have taken practice. He didn't fasten the coat, however—that must have been difficult, too, with one hand—merely picked up his walking stick from beside the desk and came and sat on the sofa beside her.

This disconcerted her, too, although he did not sit too close.

She jumped up and dragged the bag toward the sofa before falling back into her place beside him.

"I'll show you," she said, opening the bag.

He leaned forward to glance inside. "All music?"

"Apart from a little money at the bottom, which I don't want him to get his hands on either." She swallowed, feeling his gaze on her face but keeping her own on the contents of the bag. "This is my symphony. The most ambitious work I have attempted, and I think… I think it might be quite good, and I *will* not let him claim it or sell it."

"Good. Does this mean you have decided to stay and fight?"

"For now." She glanced up to find him regarding her with approval.

"Good." He sat back. "I gather he has done such things before?"

"All the time," she said ruefully. "At first, I didn't notice. I was young and silly, thrilled to be playing so often to larger and larger audiences, intoxicated by the adulation. And he did all the difficult tasks, booking concert halls and negotiating fees, publicizing… It was only gradually that I realized we never saw the fees anymore. The music I wrote vanished, only to turn up published under his name in local shops."

"Did you confront him?" Captain Gorse asked.

"He said women were not well regarded as composers, that my music sold better under a male name. That he was keeping the money safe for us. I had no reason to doubt him. We were already engaged to be married." She stopped. She had never told anyone about this before and didn't want to be doing so now. It made her too ashamed, as well as too angry. And, if she was honest, too frightened.

"And so, he grew more blatant?" Captain Gorse suggested. "Particularly, perhaps, after your mother died?"

"Even before. We traveled a good deal, and our lodgings were basic. But Gerald shared them less and less often. He would stay with some nearby nobleman, carouse all night. I know he gambled for stakes that boggled my mind. He didn't always pay up, of course, which is one reason we moved so frequently. It was when Miss Dart—my governess—confronted him about his behavior that he persuaded my mother to dismiss her. On the grounds that she had set her cap at him, which was arrant nonsense. She didn't even *like* him. When I quarreled with him over it, he said I was ridiculous, that he was looking after me. I told him it was the other way around, that it was my music that was keeping us."

She broke off and turned her face away. "I'm sorry. You don't need to hear all this."

"I think, perhaps, I do," he said.

She shook her head. "I'm sure you have gathered the important points. He cheats and he steals, and I would rather spend the rest of my life running than allow him one more penny of what I have earned. But you were right. Why should I run from the life *I* have made?"

He nodded. "I am impressed that you make enough here at Maida to live and even save what you have. But you could earn more."

"I do earn more," she confessed. "A friend in town and I write songs together and sell the music. He has a gift for fun and silly words, and I supply the music to match. They have become quite popular." She wrinkled her nose. "Of course, I have learned. We publish them under his name, but he is a good and honest man."

The captain's eyes were unreadable now. "I am glad to hear it. We may need to enlist his help at some point. But fame will earn you more."

"It has been a difficult balance," she admitted. "Finding this work at Maida saved my life, because I could play with anonymity and still earn, with little likelihood, or so I thought, of Gerald ever finding me. It has been two years, now. I had almost begun to hope that he was not interested in finding me."

"Perhaps he wasn't. He could have come upon you by accident and just decided to shake the tree, as it were, to see what fell into his lap. If you tell me everything you can about him, I'll take the information to a friend of mine and see what he can dig up."

"What friend?" she asked in sudden suspicion.

"His name is Ludovic Dunne. He is a solicitor who smells out information like a bloodhound, and he is utterly trustworthy. He was responsible for proving my brother did not commit a crime for which he would have been hanged."

Her eyes widened, and his lips quirked in response. "We all have skeletons in our cupboards, Miss Derwent. But it seems to me that both you and my brother were more sinned against than sinning. Have I your permission to consult Dunne?"

She nodded, slowly, savoring the experience of being asked and making the decision. "Is he in town?"

"Yes. I'll go this afternoon, after your concert."

She felt a flood of warmth because he still wanted to hear her, would still be there. One day, perhaps, she would tell him how much his presence had helped her. For now, she was running out of time.

"I should go." She rose reluctantly, vaguely surprised that she would have preferred to stay where she was. "Thank you," she added, nodding toward the bag.

"I could take it to town with me, leave it secure in my father's safe," he said. "Though I would suggest we leave it in Renwick's safe for now. Which reminds me, you should know Renwick is looking out for you. Monck will be closely watched if he returns here."

Curiously, that warmed her, too. Leaving him to finish dressing, she departed without feeling she had lost her dignity or her worth in the part of her story she had told him. But then, he had been to war. He must understand dignity and suffering and compassion in all their various forms.

It was not the first time she had wondered about his life, both past and present, but the need to keep a lookout for signs of Gerald stopped the speculation from overwhelming her. Instead, she noticed the friendly nods of the hotel staff that she had always taken for mere civility. If they were not close friends, at least they were acquaintances on her side. And friendship was not impossible. She had cut off so much when she had run from Gerald, which meant, in a way, that she had let him win.

The pleasure gardens were filling as she walked across from the hotel in the company of two violinists and a clarinet player. Although not the sunniest day of the year, it was still warm and the clouds light enough not to spill rain. They should have a decent audience.

While the orchestra set up on the stage, she examined her harp, which had been brought out and was waiting in the wings. From there, she could tune the harp to the rest of the orchestra and wait her turn.

Amy Laurel, a budding young soprano who had begun to sing occasionally at the midday concerts, waited with her. They nodded to each other and smiled in greeting, but it struck Natalie that the girl seemed more troubled than usual.

From the wings, she could also see the audience taking their seats, walking through the rose garden, or standing around to chat while they listened. There was no sign of Gerald. Perhaps Captain Gorse had scared him off. Or the combination of the captain, the orchestra, and Renwick. She was no longer alone, friendless, and naïve in a foreign country.

The orchestra played well, as they usually did, and toward the end of their piece, Captain Gorse walked through the gate and came to sit in his usual seat. She was aware of an extra warmth at the sight of him there today because they had spoken at last and would do so again. He had chosen to help her. And if part of her couldn't help asking cynically, *Why?*—well, the rest of her was quite happy for it to be so. She seemed to *feel* as she hadn't in years, and in spite of Gerald's reappearance, she felt good, excited about life…

The harp was moved onto the stage for her. She walked on to Amy's encouraging smile, and the orchestra stood for her. She curtseyed to them, and to the audience, and took her seat at the harp, drawing it to her shoulder before she let her gaze wander over the audience, over Captain Gorse, unsmiling but not haunted today, and then in a short, mercifully fruitless, search for Gerald.

And then the music took over, as it usually did, and the time flew by.

Usually, when she left the stage, she glanced back from the wing and saw that her officer had either vanished already or was on his way to the gate. Today, when she glanced back, he had indeed left his seat, but he was approaching the back of the stage. As, from a different direction, was Bill Renwick.

She descended the few wooden steps, and the three of them met at the foot, while the orchestra welcomed Amy onto the stage.

"Miss Natalie," Renwick said briskly, with a short bow. "My lord. A quick word."

My lord? Startled, she glanced at Captain Gorse, who did not seem remotely surprised to be so addressed.

"Shall we walk?" he suggested.

"No one has asked about you at the gate or the pavilion or the hotel," Renwick said bluntly. "So far as I know, your pursuer is not on the grounds, but not everyone saw him last night, so he might have slipped through. Until we can—er…mark this person's card properly, I would like you to have an escort whenever you go between the gardens and your cottage. The staff all know to drop what they're doing when you're ready to go home. And I'll send one of my boys to fetch you each morning. And evening when you're playing at the hotel."

"That's really kind of you, Mr. Renwick but—"

"It isn't kind at all," Renwick growled. "Protecting a valuable employee." He glanced around him. "Your bag's in my safe. Are you happy with that?"

"Yes, of course," she replied.

"And happy in your company?" he asked bluntly, staring directly at Captain Gorse, who only twisted his lips into a sardonic smile. At least, it looked sardonic, though that might have been the fault of the scar running down one side of his face and tugging at the corner of his mouth.

"Of course," she said hastily. "Captain Gorse has been most kind. And gentlemanly," she added, catching on somewhat belatedly to what Renwick was really asking her.

Renwick nodded curtly. "Until later, then. My lord."

As he stalked away, Captain Gorse said only, "Shall we walk through the gardens?"

"It's quicker from here." She glanced at him as they began to walk. *My lord?*

He shrugged. "Courtesy title. My father is a marquess, but you needn't bow before my greatness, I have three older brothers."

"Are they also cavalry officers?"

"Lord, no. Rampton, my father's heir, is in politics like him. Charles is a diplomat, William a clergyman."

"Which one was almost hanged?" she asked dubiously, though something was already tugging at her memory.

"Oh, that was Dominic, the youngest of us. And perhaps the best since he is trying to change the world."

"In what way?" she asked intrigued.

"Having personal experience of prison conditions, he is very eager to improve them."

"And you agree with him?"

"There is nothing to disagree with," he allowed.

"And yet you sound…distant. Unengaged."

"I am not engaged in any cause, being of a cynical nature."

She glanced up at him. "Because you risked everything for your country?"

"My dear lady, that isn't a cause, it's a career," he said with mock severity.

He paused for a moment, watching the antics of the stilt men who were entertaining the children along the open lawns. Which, for some reason, was when her memory clicked into place.

"Lord Dominic Gorse!" she exclaimed. "Now, I remember. He escaped from Newgate, and they thought he was here at Maida. There were Bow Street runners and Watch men running all over the gardens looking for him. And then he was proved innocent after all. Quite a tale."

"One that does not reflect well on Dominic's family." He met her curious gaze. "Incidentally, it is Dominic's lady who expressed interest in hearing you play the harp at her party."

She opened her mouth in habitual denial and then laughed. "Why not? If I am found, I no longer have a reason to hide."

"And the more powerful friends you have, the easier he will be to scare off. I could escort you to her this afternoon if you like."

Excitement surged up. New possibilities, new opportunities… And the thought of going anywhere with Captain Gorse was far too appealing.

Gerald would not win.

"Thank you," she replied. "I need to see Mr. Laurie, too—my song-writing partner—if there is time."

He nodded and they walked on. Despite his limp, he walked easily on the paths and even the tracks beyond the gardens. He even shortened his long stride to match hers. She had forgotten what a gentleman could be.

And yet as they walked, he seemed always to be quartering the area around them, including behind them. She had the feeling his every sense was alert, as it must have been in wartime. Curiously, her unease of the morning had vanished. There had been no sign of Gerald. He must already have run to torment and embezzle someone else. Which was hardly right either, damn him.

Both deep in thought, they approached the cottage in silence, though the quiet was soothing, companionable rather than uncomfortable. She liked that about him. She liked today very much.

Until she slid her key into the cottage door, and it would not turn. Blood sang in her ears. It was unlocked, and yet she knew she had been careful to turn the key fully.

"Stand aside," the captain murmured. "Wait here." To her amazement, he tugged once at his walking stick and the polished ebony casing came away to reveal a gleaming, business-like sword. He passed her the wooden cylinder with a nod and pushed open the door.

Even with Captain Gorse's body blocking the way, she could see her tidy little home was in chaos. Furniture was upended, papers strewn across the floor. And through in the bedroom, a man glanced over his shoulder and threw himself out of the open window.

"Gerald." The name broke from her in hoarse fury, even as the captain swung aside to bolt back through the front door and go after him. She leapt out of his way—which is when she saw the movement by the window.

A second, unknown man was crouching under the dining table. She doubted he was hiding there, just inspecting the underside of the table, which was no doubt why he hadn't seen them arrive. But he saw them now, for he sprang out and leapt to his feet, a blade flashing into his hands.

"Richard!" she cried, but as though sensing the danger, he had already swung back and took the man's attacking blade on his sword.

The captain had one arm and a game leg, surely negating his combat experience. She wanted to scream because this further injury, or even death, would be her fault. And because she didn't know what to do. She could not hare after Gerald, wielding the misleading scabbard like a club, not when Captain Gorse was battling this armed ruffian.

While the captain merely side-stepped the villain's next attack and contrived also to block his exit, Natalie, sidled past, circling, to come up behind the intruder. She even raised the ebony scabbard, but without warning, the ruffian's blade fell to the ground. Captain Gorse kicked it toward her while stepping forward almost casually and knocking the hilt of his sword against the man's chin. As the intruder reeled back, Gorse kicked out and yanked his feet from under him.

The man crashed down like a stone, and Captain Gorse stood over him, his sword point over the man's throat.

"Don't," the captain said. He didn't even sound out of breath. "Instead, start talking before I grow weary and feel the need to lean."

CHAPTER FOUR

RICHARD WAS WELL aware that all his advantage in a fight had been reduced to surprise. No one expected a one-armed man to put up much resistance, so he acted quickly, and so far, it had worked.

Natalie stood on the other side of the intruder, looking dazed, her hand holding his scabbard raised as though she meant to use it as a club. That pleased him. No vapors, no screaming or standing around wringing her hands. She had just looked for a way to help the situation. He was proud of her, and yet glad, somewhere, that he hadn't needed her help.

"No need for that, Captain," the intruder said cheerfully. "No intention of getting spitted for the likes of him."

"Will you close your bedchamber window, ma'am?" Richard said. "And perhaps the front door. No point in allowing your other visitor back in."

Without a word, Miss Derwent lowered the cane but kept it with her as she marched through to the bedchamber and peered out of the window before pulling it shut.

"How well do you know Mr. Monck?" Richard inquired.

"Who?"

Richard leaned very slightly. "Your partner in crime."

"Oy! Mind that thing, it's sharp!" the intruder said with what sounded like genuine indignation. "I never knew the blasted cove's name. Met him in a tavern, and he offered me a few coins to break into a cottage outside of town. Should have known better."

"You should indeed. And your name?"

Now the man really did look indignant. "Bloody officers! Don't you recognize me? I saved your sodding life at Badajoz. And you saved mine at Waterloo."

Richard frowned. He had assumed addressing him as captain was hopeful flattery, but now that he looked properly… "Daniels?"

"Praise the Lord!" Daniels said sarcastically. "Any chance I can get up now?"

"Not until you explain what you were doing breaking into the lady's home."

"I just did explain! He offered me money, and he said she was unfaithful and cheating him."

"You weren't as big a flat as to believe that."

"No," Daniels admitted. "But coin is coin."

"No one's in that much need of coin."

Daniel's lip curled with contempt but also with shame. "Yes, they bloody are."

Richard raised the sword. "Get up," he said impatiently.

Daniels spoke the truth. God knew there were enough crippled ex-soldiers and sailors in London, begging in the streets because there was no work. But if he'd told himself it was only the cripples who were without work, he'd been turning a blind eye, or at least ignoring the full truth as the lesser of two evils. If a good man was desperate enough, he'd turn to crime, too.

Daniels rose but made no effort to run as Richard had more than half-expected, and even wanted. He had no desire to deal with Daniels as a criminal and would have preferred the man made it impossible by loping off into the countryside.

Instead, Daniels began picking up the fallen furniture and putting it back in its proper place. Natalie watched him, wary and baffled.

"This is Sergeant Daniels," Richard said reluctantly. "He was one of my regiment, though not of my company. He seems to have…fallen on hard times."

"Sorry, ma'am," Daniels said with a quick, rueful grin. "Didn't know you were a friend of the captain."

"Would it have made a difference?" she snapped.

"'Course it would," he replied, shocked. He put a pile of papers on the desk and scratched his head. "Leastways, I hope it would. Afraid I was desperate and not exactly sober when I agreed. He bought me a few pints, told me some convoluted story about his wife stealing and cheating."

"This is Miss Derwent," Richard said austerely. "She is not married to anyone, and all the cheating is his."

Daniels nodded. "Backed the wrong horse," he admitted. "And didn't even get paid. At least not beyond the ale. If it makes you feel better, ma'am, he couldn't find money or anything else he wanted to steal. Although," he added, picking up some pieces of crockery from a puddle of water and flowers, "I'm afraid your vase got broken."

"I'll make tea," Natalie said tiredly, "if he's left me any crockery."

"I looked behind it," Daniels offered, "but I didn't break any." He looked uneasily at Richard. "Sorry, Captain, I shouldn't've done it. Not to anyone, let alone any friend of yours."

Richard threw himself on the righted chair and scowled at him. "How desperate are you, Daniels? Don't you have a wife? Children?"

"I'd be doing them as much good from prison as from anywhere else," he muttered. "And for all, I shouldn't have done it, I'd do worse—just not to you—to put a meal on their table."

Richard's scowl began to hurt his head. "Finish tidying up," he muttered and leaned on his sword to stand before he remembered it needed its scabbard. Daniels passed it to him.

"Sorry about the arm, sir. You still had two when I saw you last."

"Well, I almost got away with it," Richard said vaguely and limped into the kitchen after Natalie.

She had her back to him, but as he entered, he saw her hasty swipe at her eyes with her sleeve. Wordlessly, he took the step between them, propped his stick against the cupboard, and put his arm around her.

For an instant, she stiffened, and he thought she'd twist away and box his ears. Then she let go of the cracked teapot and all but fell back against him, her eyes closed, her face damp. For a moment, he just held her, his throat and heart aching. He brushed his lips across her soft, rose-scented hair, and held his rough, scarred cheek to her soft, damp skin.

Then he murmured, "He got nothing. You kept your money and your music away from him. You still have the pianoforte and your small harp undamaged."

She swallowed, and he imagined the movement of her cheek against his was a caress. Then she pulled away and lifted a cloth to remove the boiling kettle from the stove.

"The harp was knocked on the floor," she said prosaically. "One of the strings is broken."

"Then we'll buy replacements in town if you have none here."

She nodded, and he watched her pour the water into the teapot, gathering her strength back around her like a slightly tattered cloak. How often had she done this over the years? Because of the same man. Who *would* pay.

"Are you angry with Daniels?" he asked abruptly.

"Why? He's just another desperate creature manipulated by Gerald."

His lip quirked, and he had to repress the urge to kiss her cheek. "Then if you see it like that, I think he could help us."

She was putting three cups and mismatched saucers on the tray, adding a jug of cream. She nodded once, and he wished he could do something as simple as carry the tray for her. Since he couldn't, he picked up his stick and followed her back into the sitting room.

Daniels was holding the harp, frowning over its broken string. "Was that us, ma'am? I'd never have broken anything so beautiful if I'd noticed."

"It will mend," Natalie said mildly.

"Sit down, Daniels," Richard commanded.

Daniels, who seemed bemused to be given a cup of tea and a honey cake, sat on the hearth, leaving the armchair for Natalie and the hard chair for Richard. He seemed to know what was expected of him—he had always been quick—for he said at once, "He called himself Gerry, and I met him at the Bird in Hand, which is more Seven Dials than Covent Garden."

"Do you know where he lives?" Richard asked.

"No, but I had the impression it wasn't that far away."

"How did you travel out here?"

"Hackney."

Richard raised his eyebrows. "So, he's pretty flush."

"Got decent clothes," Daniels allowed.

"But probably about to run out," Natalie said cynically. "Money flows through his fingers like water."

"I can go back to the tavern and see what I can find out," Daniels offered. "I'm rightfully aggrieved since he left me to face the music alone while he scarpered. If he's not there, someone might have seen him or have a better idea where he's gone to ground."

Richard nodded. "Good plan." He stared at his boots, thinking. "Where are your lodgings, Dan? I'll come and see you tomorrow to discuss things." Then, he delved into his coat and tossed a few coins on the hearth beside the old soldier. "Get some tea and sustenance in, and if you're in touch with any of my old company who're in need of a job, bring them round, too. If Mrs. Dan won't mind."

"She'll be glad of it." Daniels, who had looked for a moment as if he'd shove the coins straight back at him, grinned and stuck them in his pocket. "Right you are, Captain." He drained his cup and glanced at Natalie, who set the plate of honey cakes beside him.

"Take them for your children," she said.

IT WAS A very odd way to make a friend, but by the time Sergeant Daniels left the cottage, she felt he was one.

"You don't ask me if I trust him," the captain observed when she had sat back down. "Given how you met…"

"I don't need to ask. I can see that you trust him."

"He made a bad choice because he is struggling. Cast adrift by the people who relied on him to fight and die in their wars. I include myself."

"You are one man."

"So is he."

"And you gave as much as anyone to the war. Anyone who survived, and I suspect you nearly didn't."

An odd expression flickered into his eyes before they fell back to his boots. Suspicion washed through her like an ache, one she doubted she could ever ask.

"I am not the only man crippled in action," he said grimly, "and far from the worst. Besides, I have enough private income to live on and a wealthy family that puts up with me. It has been four years since Waterloo. More than time for me to stop feeling sorry for myself and take back some responsibility, even if that is only a bit of extra coin for the men to help us with your erstwhile betrothed. I have an idea. I didn't mention it before, because this is your home, but it seems more valid now."

With difficulty, she followed the change of subject. "What idea?"

He frowned up at her through a fallen lock of hair, which he pushed impatiently out of the way. "I think… I think it may be some time before you feel comfortable staying here again. And it's my guess that Monck is not going to give up as easily as we had hoped. So, why don't we swap rooms?"

Her mouth fell open. "Swap?"

"You have my rooms at the hotel. We'll tell Renwick but no one else in case one of the staff let it slip. And I will stay here, ready for the next villain to try and break-in."

"But I can't," she protested. "My pianoforte is here. And in any case, I would not be allowed to disturb the other guests by playing at all hours of the night and early morning."

He shrugged. "You only need to sleep there. For the rest, this is still your home."

"Then I would have to trail up to the hotel, sometimes in the middle of the night."

"I will escort you. Or one of the men I propose to keep watch for us."

She sat back on her chair regarding him while thoughts and emotions chased around her so quickly, she could not sort them out.

"Because my music once brought you peace," she said slowly, "you do all these things for me? Though I'm nothing to you. Though you don't know me at all."

"Not *once*," he said, back to gazing at his boots. His lips twisted, and at first, she thought he had changed the subject. "I should not have gone back for the Waterloo campaign. I was already on half-pay. I had already had enough of death and killing. You'll think that odd when I had been doing it quite happily for years, but I... I began to feel ill, sick not just to my stomach but to my soul. It didn't appear to be cowardice, for I didn't mind dying. In fact, I began to look for it, almost...court it. That is what frightened me into leaving the army in 1814, even though I had once wanted a long and glorious career there. I wanted to be a general by the age of forty. Unlikely in peacetime, I know, but such are the dreams of ignorant boys."

He broke off. "I'm sorry. I should not distress you with this. It is not—"

She slid off her chair so that she knelt before his chair and took his hand between hers. "Then who else will you tell?" she asked, distressed. "You've told no one else, have you?"

He shook his head, gazing as though blind at her hands.

"Why did you return for Waterloo?" she asked gently.

"Duty," he said tonelessly. "And perhaps a glorious death. But I didn't trust myself. I asked to be on Wellington's staff, and he obliged me. My leg didn't interfere with my riding. I thought I could cope one more time. But the noise, the smell… I found no honor in what we did to each other, in what I had been doing since I was eighteen years old. It wasn't glorious. It was…obscene."

Her throat closed up. She could think of nothing to do but hold his hand to her cheek.

He didn't seem to notice. "I almost gave up and just *left*, left the battlefield. But then I found Daniels trapped beneath a horse and under enemy fire. I pulled him out, and I was able to function again. But it was only functioning. Like a machine or a clockwork toy that you wind up and point. When I was finally hit, I *welcomed* it. I'd delivered my last dispatch and had only to ride back to Wellington for more orders, but it was all over bar the shouting. The Prussians had arrived, and everyone knew Boney was done for."

She forced herself to speak, though she didn't let go of his hand. "Did you mean to be shot?"

He thought about it, which worried her. "No. I didn't even see where it came from, but it blew me off my horse. She ran off safe, so I had nothing else to worry about. I thought I was dead and was happy to be so. Until I woke up in…well, without a large part of my arm."

His eyes refocused on her face and softened. "I did not mean to tell you all this just to explain my point. Which is that when I first saw you, I was in a bad way. My body had healed as much as it could, but there was a thick melancholy I could not shift, even when I exerted myself to help my brother, something I should have been doing for weeks. And then you played."

His fingers moved in hers, but not to escape her, to touch her cheek with a wonder that almost broke her. "It wasn't just the music. It was your beauty, your simplicity, your... I cannot explain it. But you gave me courage as well as peace. And then I couldn't stay away. So yes, whatever you say, whatever you believe, there is a debt, and it is one I am happy to be able to pay. Because there is no price for what you have given me."

Her heart melted in a rush of emotion, awe, and fierce pride. She knew she should stay silent, just to remain in control and keep the overwhelming emotion in check. But she had to give him back the truth.

"Nor for what you have given me," she said huskily. "When I first saw you, I, too, was in a bad way. I jumped at sudden voices, unexpected sounds. I had no confidence in myself or my music. Gerald had told me no one came to hear the music, just to ogle me playing it. He made... He made me flirt with odious men afterward. Never more than flirt, though God knows what would have happened if I had not left him. As things were, it was enough to make me feel grubby, talentless..."

"He spoiled your dreams."

She nodded. "Playing at Maida helped a little because I was in the company of musicians. But you... At first, I thought you came to ogle, too. But often you closed your eyes, and I could see... I could see you were moved, that my music had *touched* you, that it could ease whatever haunted you. And I began to understand that Gerald had lied again. I went back to composing, to *striving*... And that, if we are talking debts, is mine to you."

A smile tugged at his lips and flickered in his eyes. "We should have spoken sooner." He had leaned forward in his chair, bending over her as she knelt at his feet, and their heads were very close together, his hand under hers, cupping her face. Too close, too intimate. Too...too right, too necessary, surely for them both.

She moved and softly kissed his rough cheek, a kiss of gratitude and friendship, letting her inhale his scent, his feel. And in return, he kissed her softly on the lips. The same kind of kiss, surely, and yet her heart surged because his lips on hers crossed an unspoken line.

Her fingers curled convulsively on his as they lay against her cheek. His eyes darkened with desire and yet it seemed to be her turn. She brushed her lips across his, and when she would have retreated, his mouth caught hers, clung, and slowly, slowly parted her lips in a long, sweet kiss that drowned her in wonder.

Gerald's kisses had been nothing like this. They had been quick, hard, all tongue and slobbering. Richard Gorse did not slobber. He tasted, he gave and coaxed, and she found herself blindly following his lead, opening wider to him in an instinctive need to be closer.

He took his hand from her face, but only to carry hers to his neck before he returned to her cheek, caressing round to her nape while the blissful kiss went on and his fingertips stroked her skin. The thrill was a little like music, tingling from her neck through her entire body, and it made her gasp. There was only this man, his kiss, his caress, and soft, warm *need*.

For a moment, he deepened the kiss and a tiny moan of pleasure escaped her. Somehow, both her arms were around his neck, her fingers lost in the thickness of his hair, while she knelt between his knees and pressed against him.

Slowly, carefully, he detached his lips from hers and drew back an inch or two. "Natalie Derwent," he murmured breathlessly, "I could kiss you forever, but that would get us both into trouble."

I don't care. Don't stop. Fortunately, the words stuck in her throat, unspoken, and she could only stare up at him mutely. His eyes were clouded yet glinted with something so exciting that she almost climbed into his lap.

But he sat back, and his knees slid back with him, leaving her leaning on one thigh. His hand stroked her hair, more comforting now than arousing.

"We are still friends," he stated, though it might have been a question.

"Better friends," she said, and thought he smiled, though she was afraid to look.

"So do you like my idea of swapping rooms?"

It took her some time to rummage her befuddled brain for the reference. And even then, it entered her head that she would be quite happy here with him. But she had discovered a great deal about him today, not least that he was a lord, the son of a marquess. They shared a bond, but one that could only ever go so far.

She drew back, sliding across the floor, and hauled herself into the other chair. Her legs seemed too weak to support her.

"I don't like the idea of you being here alone either," she managed.

"It would only be for one night until Daniels and the others can join me. And I imagine I'll be safe enough until Monck has time to recruit some other bravo."

"Then I could just stay here."

"I'm not prepared to take that chance. Why don't we have dinner at the hotel? Then you can retire to my rooms, and I shall walk back here."

She forced a rueful smile. "You galloped across battlefields under fire. I shouldn't fear for you against *Gerald*, yet I do."

"You mustn't. It would be a waste of your energies. Do you wish to change for dinner? We can then go up and tell Renwick our plans, and tomorrow we will go to town and see what we can set in motion to catch Monck."

CHAPTER FIVE

O NE OF THE hardest things Richard had ever done in his life was draw back from Natalie Derwent when she was yielding and passionate in his arms. Arm.

He had never intended it to happen. And yet he had dreamed of her sometimes when he slept, and in the wakeful, lonely nights, he had fantasized about her in his bed. The reality of the living, breathing woman was something else again. An unexpected delight aroused to sweet, heady passion, soft and beautiful and precious. And not ever someone he could take advantage of.

A vulnerable woman insulted, slighted, and robbed by the man who should have protected her. Threatened again by that same man. From what she had said, Richard's presence at her concerts had been almost as much comfort to her as to him. That pleased him, and it would have to be enough.

For now, at least.

As he lay awake the next morning in her cottage bed, wondering if she lay awake in his at the hotel, he began to think she had given him something more than comfort and trust. She had given him hope.

It was not just that he had enjoyed kissing her more than he could recall enjoying any intimacy at all for a long, long time. If ever. It was that she had caressed his scar as though it was merely part of his face. At one point, she had pressed against the stump of his lost arm without recoiling or even seeming to notice. She liked him. He had aroused her. He knew in his heart he could have taken her to bed, shown her pleasure after pleasure, and made her body sing.

But it was too quick for her. She deserved better, courtship, flowers, love. Not yet another removal of her choices.

And so, he had taken her for dinner at the hotel dining room, then conducted her to his rooms and, ignoring all temptation to stay, he had collected his few necessary things and left her with a light kiss to her fingers and a promise to meet her in the morning.

He probably imagined that her fingers had clung just a little to his respectful lips. That she had been both eager for him to stay and afraid that he would.

But today was for business. They met in the hotel foyer bright and early and walked through the gardens to the hackney stand. The morning was bright and sunny, and in her company, everything in the world seemed good. They talked in light, bantering tones, and yet he had the feeling something much more important was going on. Sometimes she blushed as she talked, as if emotion bubbled just below the surface of her petal-scented skin. He barely took his eyes off her.

His words, however, were mundane. "I'll go and visit Daniels while you are with your friend. Shall I collect you in, say, an hour? And take you to call on my sister-in-law?"

"If she would not mind."

"Of course not. She will be thrilled that I've actually done something she asked of me."

Her friend, Mr. Laurie, owned what appeared to be a music shop. A fine pianoforte was displayed in the window, and a sign invited customers to come within for an excellent selection of fine old and new instruments, and all the latest sheet music.

Richard alighted and handed Natalie down before paying the driver. He had to force himself not to escort her inside and inspect her friend and his premises. At least it was a shop and not private rooms.

"Will an hour be enough?" he asked civilly.

"Probably, but if you are kept longer, I am happy to wait."

He tipped his hat, then sauntered off down the street. He thought his limp was improving.

Daniels's lodgings were on the seedier end of Covent Garden, but the door was opened at once by a plump, tired woman with a clean apron and a generous smile. She carried a baby in her arms and another clung to her skirts.

"You must be Captain Gorse. Pleasure to welcome you to our humble abode, sir! They're waiting for you in the parlor. I'll be bringing refreshments in a mo…"

She threw open the door off the narrow hallway, "Here's the captain," she announced cheerfully and hurried off toward what looked like a kitchen, where the sound of childish, quarreling voices could be heard. The child trotting along at her skirts looked over her shoulder and grinned at him.

Richard walked into the parlor, where several men were rising to greet him, almost standing to attention.

"Captain!" they acclaimed him, grinning as though they really were pleased to see him. God knew why. Smith and Havers and Fellows from his own company. None of them were whole. Smith had lost an ear and his arm dangled at his side as if it no longer worked fully. Havers had a long, angry scar dividing his face and vanishing into his shirt. Fellows had only one leg and got about on a crutch. Richard wasn't so much appalled by their injuries as by his ignorance of them.

He'd given money to his father's man-of-business for those of his company who had been invalided out of the regiment. Why had he not seen that was not nearly enough? And still, they looked up to him.

Well, dammit, they weren't in the army now. He thrust out his hand. "Sergeant Smith. Havers. Fellows. Good to see you. Daniels, all well?"

His briskness at least got them all shaking his hand and sitting down again, two squashed onto the wooden settle, two on the empty hearthstone, and Richard on a chair.

"I've been telling them about your problem," Daniels said, "and my bad decision. Surprised the lady doesn't want to draw and quarter me."

"She knows who's to blame."

"Well, about him. He's no regular at the Bird in Hand. No one knows his name or where he stays. He only drops in occasional like. Probably when he has dodgy jobs he wants doing. And I soaked it up. But the tavern keeper will let me know if he shows up again."

"Thanks, Dan," Richard murmured. "I suspect it's only a matter of time before he threatens Miss Derwent again. And since he can't find what he's looking for, it's my belief he'll go after her person. So, she'll be staying safe elsewhere for a night, while I occupy her cottage. How are you fellows fixed for work?"

Havers shrugged. "I'm not. I scare the horses."

"And Fellows and me lost our places when old Dodger sold the livery stable," Smith said with a twisted smile. "You might say we're between work, with the *between* likely to be long."

Richard nodded. "Then you'd be available to help me out? To keep watch in the vicinity of Maida Pleasure Gardens and the cottage I mentioned? I can't tell how long the work will last, but while it does, I'll buy your rations and pay you enough that you can feed your families, too. What do you say?"

"When do we start?" Smith asked.

LAURIE HAD SOME coins to give her for the sale of song music both from his shop and others. She used some of it to buy more harp strings and then got him to help her with the piece of her symphony that wouldn't work, and she had been right. It needed the harp at that crucial place.

While she scribbled it down, she felt his gaze on her face.

"Someone was here, asking for you," he said reluctantly.

She glanced up at once. "Who?"

Laurie drew in a breath. "He said he was your husband."

Natalie went very still. "You believed him. You told him where I was."

"I told him you were playing at Renwick's Hotel on Wednesday evening. Was I wrong?"

She nodded slowly. "But you weren't to know. I never told you who not to tell, just that I preferred anonymity. We use your name on the songs, so how did he make the connection? How did he find you?"

"He said he recognized a piece, said you had played it for him."

She snorted. "I never thought he would remember it." He hadn't thought it worth stealing in Vienna. "Well, at least I know how he found me."

Laurie stood up and went to turn the Closed sign to Open. "Then you are not married to him?"

She shook her head. "We were engaged to be married once, but... I found him to be untrustworthy, so I left him and came back to England. But I knew he would follow me. Not for love, never believe that. So, I hid behind your name, behind the anonymity of Maida and Renwick's."

"I'm sorry," he said miserably. "I was trying to do the right thing."

And he was hurt, she saw, hurt by her lack of trust in him, perhaps. Or by the idea that she could have been married to another man. Not that she and Laurie had ever regarded each other as anything but friends. At least she had not. For the first time, she wondered if Laurie could possibly have harbored other feelings for her.

Richard Gorse does.

Richard Gorse was lonely, damaged. He didn't know what or who he wanted. The bond that tied them was delicate. Blooming, perhaps, but not necessarily hardy or even real.

She didn't want to think that. She wanted to melt into his arms, receive more of his sensuous kisses. More and more and more and…

Pulling herself together, she forced her mind back to Laurie's last words. *"I was trying to do the right thing."*

"I know you were," she replied kindly. "Don't worry. It turned out there was no harm done. The evening recital went very well. And since the cat is out of the bag, I no longer need to hide. I have the chance to play at a society party, which might help my career."

"Oh? Whose party?"

At that moment, the door opened, ringing the bell above it, and Captain Gorse walked in, gazing about him. Words and breath froze in her throat. For a moment, only the unscarred side of his face was visible, and he looked so handsome it gave her butterflies. There was still something of the soldier's swagger about him, even moving through a cramped shop on a game leg. She could not even say to herself that he must have been splendid before his injuries. He *was* splendid, all the more for the vulnerabilities he had revealed to her last night.

Laurie started toward him, and he turned to face him, revealing the long, pale scar. Perhaps people thought it a shame his good looks had been so marred. For Natalie, who had never seen him unmarred, it was simply part of the man whose silent presence had comforted her and intrigued her for two years. Even here, in mundane surroundings, he quickened her heart and made it ache, even as it rejoiced.

"Welcome, sir," Laurie said in his polite yet very un-servile way. "Is there something in particular I might help you with?"

At last, Natalie made her legs move forward. "Captain, allow me to present to you my friend, Mr. Laurie, the proprietor of the music shop. Laurie, Captain Lord Richard Gorse."

Laurie's eyebrows flew up, and he stiffened, even as he bowed.

Captain Gorse, however, merely propped his cane against a

cabinet of sheet music and thrust out his hand. "Very glad to make your acquaintance."

Laurie appeared to take the hand before he meant to, for he looked slightly confused.

"It is the captain's sister-in-law who has suggested I might play for her guests," Natalie said. "And the captain who is helping protect me from Gerald."

"Why?" Laurie asked.

The captain's lips quirked, although he did not seem amused. "A good question for a friend to ask," he allowed. "But I'm afraid you will have to take my word that I have no malign intent."

Laurie opened his mouth to say more. Then, perhaps recalling that it was he who had inspired Natalie's danger by revealing her whereabouts, he pressed his lips together in unhappy silence.

"Is there anything I could do to help?" Laurie asked her.

"Tell me if he comes back," Natalie suggested. "Not that I think he will, but I would be interested to know what he wants. I suppose he gave you no clue?"

"None, beyond making me believe you were his errant wife."

"Trying to deprive you of friends," Gorse said with distaste. "Isolate you. As he did before so that you have nowhere to turn but to him. He will find it a little harder, now. Are you ready to go, Miss Derwent?"

"Yes." She turned to Laurie and gave him her hand. "You have been my stalwart friend," she said quietly. "I know this." And then she turned and preceded Captain Gorse out of the shop, just as two men waited to enter. Strangers, she saw with relief, whom she had no cause to fear.

"Are you happy to walk since it is such a lovely day?" Captain Gorse suggested.

"Yes. In fact, I would rather walk. I feel I have been cooped up all day and need the exercise. How did you find Sergeant Daniels?"

"Unemployed but cheerful. He has a decent house. I can see

he would be reluctant to lose it and move to some single room or shared slum." He drew in his breath. "He was with some men of my own company, who have also fallen on hard times. I have asked them all to come and help us keep watch on the cottage and to deal with any brigands Monck might send."

"You are going to a deal of trouble, my lord."

"Since when did I become my lord?" he demanded. "And the trouble is minuscule, as well as providing an excuse to keep the men out of trouble for a few days."

"And put food on their families' tables."

"Too little, too late," he muttered.

After a short silence, she said, "I hope Laurie did not offend you. He is all the more protective for knowing he erred."

"And I'm glad to know it. Though I think he's in love with you, too."

"Don't be silly."

There seemed to be questions trying to burst out of him, but he held his peace, just walked along slightly faster, his stick clicking on the road as went.

"He might be," she allowed, "though it never struck me before today."

"He is."

She looked at him. "You want to know if I reciprocate. Though he is the only true friend I had in England for years, he has never been more and never will be. Does that answer your question?"

"I didn't ask one." He cast her a quick, crooked smile and she laughed.

LORD AND LADY Dominic Gorse lived in a pleasant house in Half Moon Street. Although unimposing by the standards of other Mayfair mansions, it seemed magnificent to Natalie after living in the cottage for so long. The servants, however, seemed a little unconventional. She was sure the butler, if such he was, was an old soldier—a straight-backed man approaching middle age but with an indefinable danger about his person. However, he greeted Lord Richard as "Captain," and made no effort to usher Natalie to the kitchens.

"Lady Dom about?" Richard asked him casually.

"In the morning room, sir."

"Don't look so awed," Richard murmured as they made their way upstairs. "It's only rented. And no, I don't have one just like it. I have rooms off Piccadilly. If you want actual grandeur, I'll take you to Sedgemoor House."

"Rented grandeur is fine with me."

With a breath of laughter, he led her down a short passage to the right and knocked on the door.

"Come in," said an impatient male voice, and Captain Gorse grinned as he turned the handle without dropping his cane and ushered Natalie inside.

Natalie had found it less daunting to walk on to a stage before a large and rambunctious audience. But she fixed a stage-smile on her face and walked in, unutterably glad that the captain followed immediately behind.

The room was occupied by only two people—a younger, more boyish version of the captain, who could only be his brother, and an obviously pregnant lady in a simple but elegant gown with her hair carelessly pinned. They both gazed expectantly at the door and then broke into grins.

"Richard, just the man we need," the lady said as though in relief.

"Well, you *might* be," said Richard's brother. "Suspending judgment while you introduce us to the lady."

"Miss Natalie Derwent," Richard said. "The harpist we spoke about, Viola. Miss Derwent, my graceless brother, Lord Dominic Gorse, and his long-suffering wife, Lady Dominic."

"I am not graceless," Lord Dominic said firmly. "And my wife copes with me very well, in moderation."

"Ignore them, Miss Derwent," the lady advised. "Do sit down here. Have you come for luncheon, Dominic? Ludovic Dunne said you'd invited him here."

"I did. And I may have forgotten to tell you," Richard said, handing Natalie into a comfortable chair. "Apologies."

"You'd be well-served if we'd gone back to the country," Dominic observed.

"Wouldn't be the first time I'd resorted to a sandwich on someone's front steps. Why are you still in town? I thought the doctors were pleased with Viola."

"They are," Lord Dominic said, sounding suddenly wrathful. "It's our glorious parent who has persuaded us to stay, and now we know why. It was nothing to do with Viola."

"Oh? What's the old devil up to now?"

Lord Dominic's gaze flickered to Natalie. "Oh, I shan't bore you with that just now."

Natalie sprang to her feet. "I should not stay. Perhaps your ladyship could send me a note if you still wish to see me. Lord Richard will give you my address—"

"Oh, no, please don't go!" It was Lady Dominic who had spoken although everyone had stood up, too. "Dominic only meant he didn't want to bore you with our family squabbles, which are legion. Why don't we leave the gentlemen to assassinate the character of their noble father while I show you our harp?"

CHAPTER SIX

"I HEARD YOU play once before," Lady Dominic said from the window, when Natalie's fingers had stilled on the beautiful, only slightly out-of-tune harp. "In Maida Gardens."

Natalie tweaked the most annoying of the strings, plucked it, and tweaked again. "I'm surprised you remember."

"I thought you were a cut above the other musicians and believed then that you could do very well through the *ton's* support. I was surprised to hear you were still at Maida to be honest."

Natalie plucked the string again and, satisfied, pushed the harp upright. "I had reasons for wishing to remain out of the public eye, while earning a living. But I thank you for the confidence."

"I am not a great hostess or patroness of the arts. But Dominic's sister-in-law, who will be present, is. Lord and Lady Wenning are invited, too, as are Mr. and Mrs. Halland." She smiled quickly. "You see I am dropping names to try and persuade you. If you still have reasons for discretion, I'm sure Richard and Dominic between them will help."

"Captain Gorse has already been most kind."

"He is looking better," Lady Dominic said, as though the realization had just hit her. "Is that your influence?"

From anyone else, it would have been insolent. From this

young woman, somehow it sounded merely pleased curiosity. Either way, Natalie had no idea how to answer.

"I don't know," she admitted.

Lady Dominic moved restlessly toward her. "Dominic says the war damaged him in spirit more than in body. And he has learned to live with the physical injuries more easily."

Natalie shifted uncomfortably but said nothing. Lady Dominic plucked the string Natalie had just tuned and smiled.

"You won't talk about him. You are loyal."

"It is not my business, your ladyship. I am a musician for hire."

Lady Dominic's eyes lifted to hers. "Oh, I think you are a great deal more. You speak like a lady, for one thing."

Natalie shrugged impatiently, for the past was always just that. "I was born into country gentry, though it no longer matters. The house and land were entailed and passed to a distant cousin on the deaths of my father and brother. My mother and I went abroad to pursue my interest in music. We thought I might earn for us by teaching a higher standard of music than the average governess. I played small concerts that grew out of social events, and then we met a man who turned it into a more commercial venture and... Well, suffice it to say he was not honest, and I returned to England with nothing but a small harp and enough for a deposit on a second-hand pianoforte. I have decided to hide from this man no longer and would welcome the opportunity to play for your guests."

Lady Dominic blinked. "Good. I hope you will also consent to be one."

"I beg your pardon?"

"Our guest," came the patient reply. "And play for us after dinner."

For the first time in years, Natalie felt tempted to accept such an invitation, and not just because she was sure Richard would be present, too. She was in danger of forgetting the station into which she had plunged herself, even before she had encountered

Gerald.

She met the other woman's gaze. "I am a working musician. I play for a fee."

"I see nothing wrong with being both guest and paid musician, and your skill can most certainly command it. Talk to Richard."

Natalie opened her mouth to retort that Lord Richard did not make her decisions and would not want to when his actual voice spoke from the doorway. "Please do talk to Richard. Dominic has deserted me in favor of the wine cellar. Have you reached agreement?"

"I have invited Miss Derwent to dine with us on the evening in question. You and she must haggle fees, for until I speak to Grace, I have no idea of such matters. Rich, your father wants Dominic to become one of his tame members of Parliament."

"So he has just told me. It would certainly give him a platform to promote prison reform."

"That is what I said, and your father is prepared to tolerate that, but Dom says he won't vote to please him."

"Good for Dom," Richard drawled. He glanced at Natalie. "My father is a shocking old reactionary. Dominic, however, could do a lot of good from the inside."

Lord Dominic himself appeared in the doorway with a bottle swinging from either hand. "Are we gathering in here? Why not? A glass of sherry, Miss Derwent?"

A manservant followed their host into the room, depositing a tray of glasses.

"Might do you good, Dom," Richard pointed out. "He'll fund you, and there's nothing he can do if you vote against him. Not until the next election at least."

Dominic presented a glass of sherry to Natalie with an unexpectedly sweet smile and gave another to his wife. "The trouble is, I would make a terrible representative. I wouldn't be bothered with the concerns of my constituents, which I know I'd see as largely petty and silly. I would pursue prison reform and ignore the rest, and that's no better than any other member with a vested interest."

"It sounds less selfish," Natalie pointed out, and Richard gave a crack of laughter.

Dominic glowered at his brother as he clinked glasses with him. "You do it, then."

"He doesn't want me, Dom," Richard said quietly. "I'm the soldier, and I've done my bit. You're the one he let run riot, and now you're fit enough to be tamed. It's your reward for not going to war."

Dominic threw himself onto the sofa beside his wife. "I'm not steady enough, Rich. And I don't want to be. I can do more from outside the establishment."

"Then tell him."

"I did. When have you ever known that to deter Sedgemoor? Greetings, Dunne," he added as another tall man with almost white-blond hair strolled into the room. "Not that you're unwelcome, but why are you lunching with us?"

"Lord Richard told me I was," came the immediate response. "Lady Dom, how are you? You look blooming."

"Thank you, kind sir!" Lady Dominic smiled as he bowed over her hand. "Allow me to introduce you to our other guest. Miss Derwent, this is Mr. Dunne, our very good friend and solicitor extraordinaire."

Lord and Lady Dominic were either casual or thoughtful hosts, because before the sherry was even consumed, they had both wandered off, leaving Mr. Dunne alone with Richard and Natalie.

On closer inspection, despite the whiteness of his hair, Mr. Dunne was younger than she had thought. He could not have been much over thirty. His expression was patient and amiable, although his grey eyes were shrewd as they passed from Richard to her and back again.

Richard said abruptly, "Are you happy for me to tell Mr. Dunne what we discussed?"

Natalie gripped her fingers together in her lap and nodded once. Silly to be ashamed when she had done nothing wrong, but she could not help it. She gazed at her hands while Richard succinctly explained what Gerald had done in Europe and how he had behaved since finding her at Maida.

"If we could catch him, we could charge him with house-breaking," Mr. Dunne offered. "If both you and his accomplice will testify against him. The trouble there, of course, is that your friend will stand trial alongside him, so we might be better to let that go and catch him in the next attempt."

"My fear is," Richard said carefully, "that his next attempt will be on Miss Derwent's person. We need a means of compelling him to leave her alone." The men exchanged glances. Was it some kind of male code for "seeing him hang"?

"You want me to investigate him here and abroad?" Mr. Dunne asked.

"If you please," Natalie said suddenly, lifting her gaze. She was damned if she would allow Gerald to destroy her life a second time, especially now that Richard was…here.

"I can make inquiries in England immediately," Mr. Dunne said. "Abroad will obviously take longer and I will need details from you, Miss Derwent about the places you stayed and the people you met. In fact, if people you met abroad are now back in England, that may save us some time."

Natalie frowned. "There is Miss Amelia Dart, my old gover-ness who traveled with us. Gerald persuaded my mother to dismiss her. And there was Dr. Swinton, a traveling Scottish physician who treated my mother. I don't know whether either of them returned home, but I imagine they would have had to, eventually."

Mr. Dunne took a notebook from inside his pocket, spread it open at a double blank page, and passed it to Natalie. "Write everything down, and everything you know about these people."

OVER LUNCHEON WITH the Gorses, Natalie began to relax at last. The eccentric aristocrats were not so different from people she had been brought up amongst. Though their lineage might have been grander, so was their humor and their acceptance.

Oddly, as she grew more comfortable, Richard became quieter, more thoughtful. However, at least her anxious examination could find no trace of the black, haunted look she had seen so often before. And a man was allowed to think.

In all, it was a surprisingly pleasant meal. Even fun, for she found herself warming to Richard's brother and sister-in-law, and even to Mr. Dunne who turned out to be remarkably amusing for a solicitor. So it was with some reluctance that she eventually murmured to Richard, "I think I must return to Maida. I should practice for tonight's concert. But you do not need to—"

He rose at once and began to make their farewells. Although she had been prepared to go back alone, she was glad of his company. But more than that, she could not recall the last time anyone had ever done anything simply because she asked it.

In no time, they were on the landing, with their hosts and Mr. Dunne. The strange butler, whose name was Napper, was leading three more men of fashion upstairs.

"Lord Calton, my lady, with friends." He didn't sound entirely approving, though the Gorses all greeted the handsome Lord Calton with amiable banter. Clearly, he was a favorite among them.

"Forgive the rudeness, Lady Dom," Calton returned with a smile that was probably devastating to most women. Even Natalie was not entirely immune. "These fellows are clinging to me like limpets because they want me to fleece them at the newest gaming club. I said I'd go if Dom was free to join us, which he clearly isn't. But where are my manners? May I present, Mr. Davenport and Mr. Monck."

Natalie saw him, like a recurring nightmare, even before Lord Calton spoke the name. Her hand reached out blindly toward Richard before she realized the stupidity. They were in public, and in any case, he needed his hand for his walking stick. But before she could snatch it back, his fingers found hers and squeezed. And he drew her an inch closer to his side.

"Gentlemen, Lord and Lady Dominic Gorse," Calton was saying with a flourish, and both men bowed to her ladyship. If Gerald had seen her, if he had always known she was here, he gave no sign of it. "Captain Lord Richard Gorse and…" The smile dawned again. "Sadly, I am unacquainted with this lady, a failing which I do hope you mean to rectify, Lady Dom."

"My friend, Miss Derwent," her ladyship said graciously though with just a hint of warning, probably aiming to protect her from Calton's clear intention to flirt. If only she had known that was the least of Natalie's worries.

"My dear Lady Dominic," Gerald said, stepping toward Natalie, pinning her with his brightest, strongest gaze. "There is no need to introduce my wife to me."

The blood sang in her ears, as despair and helpless fury all but overwhelmed her. Even though he had told Laurie she was his wife, she had never imagined he would dare claim her as such in public. But she saw that it was perfect. In public, she could not deny it without causing a scene, and as his wife, she would have to go with him.

She even saw the triumph surge into his eyes, which, now she was close enough, she saw to be rather more bloodshot than she recalled. The lines around his eyes were deeper, too, the shadows darker, and his pallor was too pasty to be healthy. The skin had begun to sag on his face. He was losing his good looks.

There was an instant when everyone gazed at her in surprise, and she wanted the floor to open beneath her and swallow her. Lord and Lady Dominic would think she had lied. Mr. Dunne would think… Where was Mr. Dunne? He seemed to have vanished and God help her, that did not matter. Richard no longer held her hand. *What do I do?*

Richard laughed, a totally unexpected sound of easy amusement. "In your dreams, Monck, in your dreams. Such an amusing fellow. You will excuse us, Viola, I must escort Miss Derwent to her next appointment. Good day, all."

Suddenly, her feet could move again. With Richard shepherding her, it seemed she was more than capable of casting a last smile at her hosts, walking between Lord Calton and Gerald, and beginning a stately descent of the stairs.

Behind them, she heard Lord and Lady Dominic herding everyone into the drawing room for tea.

⟫⟫⟫⫷⫷⫷

SHE COULD NOT speak until they sat in the hackney, clopping through the London streets, alongside Hyde Park. Only then did she realize he had allowed her silence, respected it.

"It is not true," she blurted. "I never married him."

"Good."

She stared at him. "Just *good?*"

His lips quirked. "Good is a start. It was quite clear what he was doing, but it would be harder to refute if it were true."

"You headed him off very well," Natalie said admiringly. "He won't be able to bring it up again without seeming either a bore or a husband who can't keep his wife in line. But I hate to think of Lord and Lady Dominic being forced to entertain that *insect.*"

"Oh, Dom never does anything he doesn't want to do. In this case, he'll find out what he can in Monck's company."

"He won't go gaming with him, will he? Gerald cheats."

"Of course, he does," Richard murmured.

"And he is not fit company for Lady Dominic, who is too kind—"

"And too shrewd to fall for his lies. Dunne is there, too, remember? He slipped into the morning room to watch, knowing his name might frighten the inestimable Monck."

"Then he will still investigate?" she asked hopefully. "He won't be put off by Gerald's claim that I am his wife?"

"Nothing puts Dunne off."

She felt her shoulders relax. "And those men with Gerald? Do you think they are under his thumb?"

"I don't know the Davenport fellow, but Calton has never been under anyone's thumb, and I don't see him starting with a cheating nonentity like Gerald Monck. My dear, nothing has changed. He made another ploy and lost."

"I think he is ill," she said. "He does not look well. I wonder if that is why he is reduced to trying to force me back to him?"

"Too much dissipation will make a man look like that. Unfortunately for him, it also makes tricking people out of their hard-earned money somewhat harder. Since his looks are fading, he is relying on reviving your old fear of him. Don't let that happen."

"I won't." And she didn't believe she would. There had been enough time for anger and hatred to overwhelm the fear. Usually. And besides, seeing him today, he was somehow…diminished.

"But I will allow him determination," Richard said thoughtfully. "It can't have been coincidence that brought him to my brother's house. He must have troubled to find out my name and insinuate himself in circles that know me."

She leaned forward urgently. "You must take care. He does not play by any rules."

"Neither do I, as it happens."

She shook her head. "Yes, you do. You are just prepared for those who don't." Another thought had struck her during her silence. "If he suspects I might be looking toward playing in society, he will try to ruin my reputation with Lady Dominic. And from her to everyone else. He could blacken your name, too, linking it to mine."

"My reputation would only shine from such a link. I shall be duly flattered."

CHAPTER SEVEN

B Y THE TIME they returned to the cottage, Richard's old soldiers, including Daniels, had arrived. They lined up for inspection, and Richard introduced each of them by name. As apparently instructed, they had brought provisions for Natalie as well as themselves. While she cooked something for the men, Richard bowed and departed for the hotel.

She could not help being disappointed. But then, if Gerald did try to tarnish their reputations, Richard would not wish to give too much fuel to rumor. After all, they were already sleeping in each other's room—admittedly apart—and traveling together in closed carriages. If Natalie had been a debutante, or even back in her old life in the country, she would already be ruined.

The men insisted on eating outside. While they did so, Natalie replaced the broken string on her slightly battered harp and settled down to practice. Although she did her best, at times like these she missed not having the full-sized harp constantly with her. But that instrument belonged to her employer, and besides, there was no room in her tiny room for a large harp as well as the pianoforte.

When she had changed and dressed her hair for the evening, she emerged cautiously from the cottage. Before she had even locked the door, her escort materialized at a respectful distance on either side. Smith, with one ear, and Havers with the horrific facial scar. The latter wore a wide-brimmed hat, pulled down to cover most of his face.

"We'll walk behind you, Miss," Smith said. "Don't look back unless you hear us call to you, just trust we'll be there. Daniels and Fellows will keep the cottage safe."

"Lovely music, ma'am," Havers muttered. "Does the heart good."

She smiled her pleasure in his remark and set off along the track.

An hour later, her second evening recital began. Captain Gorse sat in his usual place, his posture relaxed, his eyes watchful. And not haunted. The orchestra played their hearts out. So did Natalie, for him.

And nowhere in the audience did she see Gerald. All was right with the world.

GERALD MONCK WAS in fact at Renwick's Hotel but keeping a low profile in the less exclusive wing, where he had contrived to encounter Amy Laurel. When they met in the coffee room, which doubled as a refined kind of taproom, she looked delighted to see him. Monck was actually flattered until he realized more of her attention seemed to be on a younger man brooding by the empty fireplace. Clearly, she was using Monck to make this person jealous.

A girl after my own heart. Monck chose to be amused rather than annoyed.

"Not at the concert, sir?" she said.

"I thought I might catch the final piece."

"I caught the first," she admitted. "She's very good is our Miss Nat."

"Then why on earth does she stay in that peasant's cottage?" Monck was only making conversation. He didn't expect to learn anything important from the remark.

So, he was surprised when Amy said carelessly, "Well, she don't no more."

Monck stilled, his ale halfway to his mouth. "She no longer lives at the cottage?"

"Got a room here now."

Damn, that would make it harder to get to her since Renwick was making it his business to guard her. "Then why does she go to the cottage?"

Amy looked coy. "Goes to meet that captain, don't she?"

Perhaps she did. Though Monck's instincts told him she was far too straitlaced for such an affair. It was much more likely they had swapped rooms to fool him. But that was an obstacle for later contemplation. For now, he had to get into the other wing of the hotel without being stopped and ejected by Renwick's un-gentle henchmen.

"I believe I'll toddle over to the concert, now," he said, finishing the ale he had no intention of paying for. "Is there a door from here to the other wing of the hotel?"

"Yes, but it's locked. Only staff got the key."

He smiled at her. "Well, you are staff, are you not?"

She eyed him uncertainly.

He winked. "Think how jealous it will make that young man over yonder if you leave with me? Then you can return and make his evening."

Amy laughed. "You are terrible mischievous, sir!"

"Oh, I am, I am," Monck agreed, offering his arm as though she were a lady and worth the courtesy.

NATALIE PLAYED SO well that it should have reduced Richard to tears. As indeed her music had in the past, however secretly. Tonight, he was too watchful to lose himself completely. He sat slightly to one side, as though for the best view of the harpist at the center of the stage, though it had the added benefit of allowing him to see most of the audience, too.

From the door, Renwick would be watching the rest. He had agreed to admit Monck, but to let Richard know as soon as the man arrived. If he arrived.

Part of Richard wanted him to turn up so that they could beat the matter out immediately. The other half wanted the evening for Natalie's triumph alone. To enjoy her company in peace. To bask in the new, disturbing happiness she brought to him.

Richard had always appreciated women, had derived considerable pleasure from many. But even before his injuries, no one had ever affected him like Natalie Derwent. It was as if he had spent two years getting to know her without ever exchanging a word, for she seemed to be as necessary to him now as breathing, an impossible combination of familiarity and mystery.

Faithful to his habit, he rose on her last note. Her gaze flew to him, her stage-smile fixed until he inclined his head and let his own smile break out. And then she shone, and his heart ached with pleasure and hope, just because he could affect her so.

He made his way down the hall toward the doors, which were now open. Renwick still stood there.

"He's in the foyer," he murmured as Richard passed.

Richard nodded curtly. There was no point in being annoyed, and this way, perhaps, the whole business could be ended all the quicker. But he didn't have to make it easy for Monck. As he had always meant to, he swung immediately left toward the musicians' room and was aware of Monck, on the periphery of his vision, hurtling toward him.

Monck caught him at the door, mainly because Richard allowed it. For he had no intention of letting Monck near Natalie.

"My lord." Monck bowed punctiliously. "Might I beg the favor of a word?"

Richard regarded him consideringly, with something of the look he had once accorded over-cocky recruits. He waited until

Monck's feet shifted and the man's hand lifted toward his cravat as though to loosen it.

"Very well," he allowed in a bored voice and turned, indicating a public room on the other side of the foyer. An elegant sign proclaimed it to be the *Gentlemen's Sitting Room*, and fortunately, it was empty. Richard sat in the nearest chair and waved Monck to the one opposite. "Come to the point, if you please."

"Very well. I gather you did not believe my statement this afternoon, that the lady you believe to be Miss Derwent is, in fact, Mrs. Monck."

"You are entirely correct."

"I am sorry to see an honorable gentleman such as yourself— a marquess's son, a hero of the late wars—tricked by my wife. I am ashamed."

"We will leave the reasons for your shame until later. I still await your point."

"My lord, whatever she has told you, she is my wife. Of course, your station in life is so immeasurably above ours that you may not care. But I do. I am prepared to forgive my wife. I want her to return to me, assured that I shall never, in word or deed, castigate her for leaving me. Even though she left me for another man."

Richard kept his face carefully devoid of any expression except that of cold amusement.

"She did not tell you that?" Monck guessed. "His name is Laurie. He owns a music shop now. He may have inherited it, I'm not sure. Nor do I know whether he discovered her true nature, or she decided—"

"Then if you do not know, there is little point in wasting time in speculation," Richard remarked. "In fact, you will also forgive me for pointing out that everything you say is worse than speculation. Mere allegation without proof. Your word against hers." Richard smiled. "And against mine. You will not win a war of reputations, Monck. I cannot advise you strongly enough against it."

"I would not dream of such a thing." The man sounded genuinely shocked. He reached inside his coat and brought out a folded document which he offered to Richard. "Proof, my lord. Of my marriage to Natalie Derwent."

Leaving his cane propped between his leg and the table, Richard unhurriedly took the document and unfolded it.

"Marriage lines," Monck explained, in case, presumably, Richard was too stupid or too emotional to be able to read it for himself. "The wedding was conducted by an English, Protestant clergyman, in a village near Rome and duly witnessed, as you see."

Richard folded the document, placed it in his own pocket, and rose with the aid of his walking stick. "Thank you for this evidence."

For the first time, alarm glimmered in Monck's eyes. He leapt to his feet, facing Richard. "My lord, it was not a gift! I merely show you it for courtesy's sake—"

"Then I shall return it to you in due course. With equal courtesy."

"Now would be better. I need it to bring my wife back to me!"

"You need it to threaten her and bamboozle other people," Richard uttered with contempt. He made a move toward the door, but Monck side-stepped into his path.

"My document," Monck said with no pretense of amiability now. Although he was not as tall as Richard, he had the advantage of two steady legs and two arms. And an ugly look about the mouth, which Richard had no time for.

Richard brought up the knob of his cane and shoved Monck sharply in the chest. Monck staggered back in surprise, clutching at the sudden pain.

"Keep your distance, sirrah." With a curl of the lip, Richard stalked past him and out the still-open door.

Monck caught up with him in the foyer. "Forgive me, my lord, I meant no disrespect. I am over emotional as I'm sure you can understand. Of course, you mean to confront my wife with this evidence, as is only right, and of course, your word to return it is quite enough for me."

By this time, Richard had led him straight to the front door of the hotel. The doorman kindly opened it, and Richard walked through, Monck at his heels.

"Good night, Mr. Monck." Richard waited only long enough to be sure that Havers, lurking near the other door to the cheaper wing of the hotel, had heard him, then turned on his heel and walked back across the foyer.

Natalie could not help feeling a touch disappointed that Richard didn't come immediately to the room next to the stage. She had wondered if they might have dinner together again... Although she suspected it cost a fortune to dine at Renwick's.

Mr. Renwick himself came to speak to her. "Congratulations, Miss Nat. These recitals seem to be going very well. Several people have asked about you, you know. We might consider a small reception after the next concert if you don't hate the idea. To let your adoring public meet you in person."

"Oh, no," she said at once. It reminded her far too much of the after-concert receptions Gerald had organized, where she had been put on display for lustful men to ogle. Although nothing untoward had actually happened, she had felt both unsafe and humiliated.

"Well, think about it." Renwick sounded disappointed, but he didn't press her, probably because Richard had entered the room at last.

He looked distracted, although his frown vanished when he saw her. And suddenly, life was wonderful again.

He did indeed sweep her off to the dining room, and her troubles seemed to fall away. She did not even think about the future, except for a vague, pleasantly excited feeling, or about the past. The present consumed her, filling her with gladness in her company and an ever-increasing physical awareness that actually made her shiver when their fingers brushed by accident. And when they stood and he lightly placed her shawl about her shoulders, a delightful little thrill ran down her spine.

Without asking, he escorted her upstairs to her rooms. *His* rooms. A strange, heavy warmth tingled low in her stomach. She walked along the passage at his side, her hand lightly on his sleeve, moving with his walking stick, which he was barely leaning on at all.

I don't want him to leave me, she thought suddenly. *How do I make him stay just ten minutes longer?* And then, *Will it be any easier in ten minutes?*

Idiot. You will see him again tomorrow.

Still, by the time the door to her—his—rooms stood open, she wanted to lock her arms around his neck and bury her face in his throat, inhale the warm, earthy scent of his skin...

Such feelings were new to her, wonderful, and yet just a little frightening. And in her heart, she knew she could not act upon them. She walked past him and turned to say good night—and found he had followed her inside and now stood toe to toe with her.

She could not breathe, even with her lips parted to speak the words which had deserted her. The sheer, masculine beauty of his face, scar and all, made her want to weep. The urge to touch him was irresistible, except her body seemed too boneless to move. His normally ice-hard blue eyes were warm and clouded and focused intently on her mouth, and her insides dissolved into molten heat.

"You will allow me to look around the rooms?" he said, his voice husky although he dragged his gaze and his person away from her, all but striding around the room, lighting candles, poking at the curtains with his stick, and then moving through into the bedchamber, where he went through similar procedures, and even looked in the wardrobe. She knew he did because she heard the doors open and close while she remained rooted to the same spot he had left her, listening to the quick, loud thuds of her own heart.

If she didn't move, he would think she was just waiting for him to leave.

I am. I am waiting for him to leave.

He came back into the sitting room. "Better safe than sorry," he murmured, approaching her. "Are you comfortable enough here without your own things?"

"I like it," she blurted. "The bed smells of you."

Appalled at her own words, she could only stare at him defiantly. But he didn't seem offended.

His lips quirked upward in his characteristic almost-smile. "So does yours."

An oddly tense and yet sweet silence stretched between them.

Then he stepped closer and bent his head, brushing his lips against her cheek, sending warm sensation scattering through her veins. "Good night, Natalie."

She forced her voice to work. "Good night, Richard." Greatly daring. She stood on tiptoe, aiming for his own cheek in return.

He cheated. Whether by accident or design, he moved, and her lips connected with his for the briefest moment. Instead of jumping back in alarm, she brought up her hand to touch his cheek, pleading, though for what, she could not have said.

"If I kiss you," he said, low, "you will have to order me from the room because I suspect that is the only way you'll get me to leave."

"You have already kissed me."

"No," he said, incomprehensibly. "No."

His mouth covered hers, seemed to sink into her lips, and fuse. A sound almost like a sob escaped her because this, *this* was what she truly wanted. A lover's kiss, *this* lover's kiss, one that invaded and worshipped, bringing pleasure and desire in equal measure. So lost was she in the experience that she didn't know if she had pressed herself so tightly against him, or if his arm had swept her there. But every inch of her from breasts to thighs sang with delight to be so close to his hard, male body, to feel the wicked column of his erection against her abdomen while his mouth plundered and seized and demanded her response.

She gave it with helpless abandon, both arms around his neck, one hand clutching at his hair, the other roaming down his lean back to the swell of his rear. He began to move against her like a whole-body caress. His knee parted hers, and she gasped into his mouth as his thigh touched the hot tenderness that was suddenly the center of her need.

"Make me go," he whispered against his lips. "Command me. Hit me. Or just ask, I'll obey, but please, please do it quickly…"

"Stay," she whispered back. "Please."

He drew back, his breathing quick and uneven. "Do you even know what you're asking?"

"No." She didn't know whether to laugh or cry. "Yes, sort of. I don't… I only know it has to be you."

He stared down into her eyes, still holding her to him with one arm. Then his head bent, and very gently, sweetly, he kissed her again. For a moment, she feared it was a farewell kiss, for his hand slid up to detach hers from his nape, but he didn't let go, merely turned and led her to the bedchamber.

She knew another moment of panic when he returned to the sitting room, but then through the doorway, she saw the light fade as he snuffed the candles. She had no idea what to do, a realization that brought about a quite different panic. Until he walked back into the bedchamber, propped his cane by the bed, and blew out the candles, leaving only the pale glow from the lamp nearest the bed.

"I never felt this for anyone before," she blurted. "Not even Gerald when I was at my most infatuated."

He raised his hand and began drawing pins from her hair. "I don't come to you a pure or chaste man," he said. "There have been women, women I have cared for. Would you believe me if I said they don't hold a candle to you, here with me now?"

She shook her head, smiling ruefully, and he ran his fingers through her loose hair, pushing it behind each shoulder before he touched her lips. "Then I shall have to prove it to you. Somehow."

His lips took hers once more, while his fingers found the fastenings of her gown. It couldn't have been easy one-handed, though the insight never entered her head until the gown sagged off her shoulders and he bent to trace the line of her clavicles with his mouth. While he kissed, he untied her chemise, and then, in a courtly gesture, he took her hand and urged her to step away from her clothes.

She stood before him naked but for her stockings and garters. Heat surged through her, much of it embarrassment, but also a strange, powerful arousal as his eyes drank her in so greedily. She stepped nearer him to hide. At least, she thought that was her intention, but somehow, she was unbuttoning his coat with trembling, determined hands, and pushing it off his shoulders. It landed on the floor, but he didn't seem to care. His hand reached behind her and pulled her naked hips to him to let her feel his arousal through his pantaloons.

Another of those small, inarticulate sounds escaped her throat. She removed his cravat pin and tossed it on the dressing table before untying his cravat and letting it fall on his coat. Because she wanted to, she buried her nose in his neck, kissed his throat while his hand caressed her naked back, and his heart beat fast and strongly against her breasts.

Impatient now, she began tugging his shirt from his pantaloons, eager to pull it off and touch the rest of him, skin to skin.

But he caught her hand. "Wait. Let me douse the lamp."

"Why?" she whispered, inhaling him, burrowing beneath his shirt.

"Because the sight will shock you more even than the touch. And I don't want to stop."

She paused, the meaning of his words penetrating her haze of lust and pleasure. His sheer vulnerability took her breath away.

"I want to see you," she whispered. "All of you."

"You don't."

She kissed his throat, her lips stretching into a smile against his skin. "I do." With a little push, she persuaded him to sit on the bed, and then she drew the shirt up over his head.

His chest was broad, smooth, and muscled, with a faint scattering of coarse blond hairs, a tempting line of which ran away from his navel into his pantaloons. She swept her fingers over the expanse of his chest, over his thickly muscled shoulder and right arm. Awed, she smoothed her palm over to the other shoulder and down the short stump of his arm. He sat tense and unmoving.

She swallowed. "Does it hurt?"

He shook his head. So, she kissed what was left of his arm. He flinched, but she continued kissing up to his shoulder and chest until his tension seemed to leak away, and he lay back on the bed. She followed, stretching out upon him in languorous, decadent bliss. He smiled against her lips when she kissed him, and then rolled her beneath him.

Excitement soared in her because he was taking charge, because he would show her the way. There was a good deal of breathless wriggling while he kicked off his pantaloons and stockings, and then his fingers and his mouth were everywhere on her, driving everything but helpless lust from her mind. He pleasured her breasts with his lips, while his hand caressed her knee and thigh and swept inward and upward to her most intimate places.

If it had not felt so wonderful, so right, perhaps she would have been shocked. As it was the sharpness of the thrill made her gasp with delight. And from there, it only got better as he explored and stroked, and then it was not his fingers but something much larger that nudged and stroked and slid its way into her body.

She cried out in wonder and need. He pushed further, filling her, and then stilled, his breath coming in short pants as she tried to hide the discomfort.

"Oh, sweetheart," he whispered, resting his forehead against hers. "Let me show you…" He kissed her, stroked her until she relaxed once more, and the glow of desire surged back with a vengeance. Only then did he begin to move inside her, tenderly, relentlessly guiding her through all the wonder and bliss of which her body was capable. Leading her to joy.

CHAPTER EIGHT

SINCE WATERLOO, THERE had not been many women in Richard's life. None before or after had given him such intense pleasure as the virgin he made love to in Renwick's Hotel.

He had imagined, somehow, that she would be experienced to some degree, that she would have known some intimacy at least with her one-time betrothed. That Monck would have used physical pleasure, to say nothing of her ruin, to bind her to him. At first, Richard had even wondered if Monck had just been an appalling lover to teach her so little of fleshly delights. But then he *knew*.

Richard was her first lover. As he fell asleep in her arms, he wondered, vaguely, if he would have taken her had he known. If he should be ashamed. But he wasn't. He was fiercely, gloriously glad.

She was his, and he would protect her and keep her.

I love her, was his last conscious thought. And his first when he awoke.

Since they had not bothered to shut the bed curtains, the early dawn light played across the pillow where she lay under his arm. She looked so beautiful and peaceful that his heart ached. His morning arousal tempted him quite sorely to wake her to a little more love before he left.

No experience in his life could better that of her coming apart in his arms, not once but twice. Her awakening to passion, her joy, moved him beyond expression. And he wanted to show her more. He wanted to take more. To spend the day here, just making love to her with the odd meal and drink to sustain them.

But she needed sleep and rest from him. And he had to think of the future as well as the intoxicating present.

He could not go on drifting and doing nothing except feeling sorry for himself, being only occasionally roused to pursue some goal, like Dominic's innocence, before lapsing back. Natalie and her music had roused him from his torpor and given him a greater goal, though it was a largely selfish one. He had other responsibilities. He had to look after his men. There was a whole world of injustice and neglect out there. And he had to look after Natalie if he meant to make a life for them both.

While the sun rose, snippets of ideas that had been fluttering into his head over the last few days now joined and clarified in his mind. Slowly, reluctantly, he lifted his arm from Natalie. She made a faint, sleepy sound of disapproval, but did not wake. He slipped away from her heat, got out of bed, and climbed with difficulty into his clothes and boots.

Then he quietly left his room and the hotel and went to confer with the men at the cottage. Half an hour later, he begged a cart ride into town from a local farmer and was dropped off in town near St. Paul's. After a conversation with the family solicitor, he set off in the direction of Dunne's offices. Only then, he recalled he had changed his coat. The marriage lines were still in his evening coat in his room at Renwick's.

Annoyed with himself, he changed direction toward the livery stable where two of his men had worked until last week.

"Where are the horses?" he asked the old man who lumbered down to greet him from the house behind the stables.

"Sent them to another stable to be sold. My buyer doesn't want the horses."

"Who is your buyer?"

"Name of Manners. Wants to tear all this down, including my

house, which is a perfectly good house in a modest way, and build something new. Houses, shops."

"Have you no one to carry on your own business?"

"Nah. Only the one daughter and she married a farmer over in Hertfordshire. Going to live with them once I get shot of this place."

Richard pounced. "Then you are not yet shot of it?"

"Negotiating over price," came the lugubrious response, from which Richard gathered that the buyer was offering a pittance. "And God knows how long the horses will take to sell. Most of them are getting long in the tooth, too."

"Do me a favor," Richard suggested. "Don't sell for a couple of days. I might make you an offer myself, to include the horses. And I won't pull your house down."

⟫⟫⟫✳⟪⟪⟪

NATALIE COULD NOT recall ever waking with such a sense of well-being and happiness.

Richard.

Captain Lord Richard Gorse, her haunted soldier, was her lover. Her whole body tingled with remembered delight. With shy yet sensual languor, she turned over to embrace him. And found she was alone.

The disappointment was acute, though she supposed he might be preserving her reputation. On the other hand, they should probably be more worried about the damage caused by her staying in his rooms at the hotel, even if he was not in them at the time. It would only take one of his friends or a member of his family to come knocking and find her here.

She smiled because she found it hard to care. Rising from the bed, she went to find her watch. She would need to be quick if she wished to return to the cottage and prepare for the midday concert. She used Richard's washing water, then slipped on her easily fastened old work dress, which she had left here for just this purpose.

The evening gown in which she had performed, still lay on the floor where it had fallen last night. Blushing with delicious memory, she picked it up and shook it out before rolling it up with her other things and bundling it into her shawl to make a parcel.

Then she tidied up the room, retrieving Richard's tossed-aside clothing and putting them away. The man needed a valet. He must struggle unnecessarily with only one hand to fasten so many buttons and tie his cravat. But she suspected that was part of the reason he did without help. To force himself to learn. She would ask him when she returned to the cottage, for she suspected he was there, waiting to accompany her to the gardens.

Something rustled under her feet. A document that must have fallen from Richard's pocket. She bent to pick it up, catching it by one corner and it flapped open. As often happens, her own name caught her gaze, and she stared in horror at the certification of a marriage between herself and Gerald Monck.

Her hand flew to her cheek. How long had Richard been in possession of this? At the very least, he must have had it last night when he took her to dine, when he came with her here. Was that why he had made love to her? Because he imagined she was, as a clearly unfaithful wife, available?

No, no, she would not let the beauty of last night be sullied by such a sordid explanation. Nor could she believe Richard capable of such cynicism.

Who are you trying to lie to? she lashed herself. *Of course, he is cynical. Jaded, disillusioned, angry…*

But not with me, a tiny voice pleaded inside her mind. *Surely not with me…*

And yet, why else would he have said nothing about this? Where had he got it from?

Gerald, of course. It had to be Gerald.

Her mind in a whirl, she managed to concentrate enough to leave the hotel with discretion and walk to the cottage.

It, too, was empty, although Daniels appeared at the door only a moment after she had closed it, to report that all was quiet and that the captain had gone into town. Frustration threatened to tear her apart. She wanted—*needed*—to see Richard, *now*. She had to know if Gerald had been able to pollute even this.

"I won't let him," she whispered fiercely to her harp. "I won't."

The question was if she had any choice in this either.

HE WASN'T IN his usual place when she waited just offstage. Smith and Havers had accompanied her to the gardens and melted away. She felt sick. She wondered if she would ever see him again, if he would ever know…

She walked onto the stage and curtseyed as usual before sitting at the harp. Another desperate glance showed her the still-empty seat at the front. There was only one thing she could do. Play.

And when, reluctantly, she came to a close and looked up from her harp, Richard sat in the seat at the far left of the front row.

She had to close her eyes for a moment as the emotion of the music clashed with the sudden flood of relief and fresh fear and sheer, overwhelming love. And then, forcing herself, she stood and curtseyed to the audience and to the orchestra, and walked off the stage. Her legs trembled so much, she all but collapsed onto the waiting stool beside Amy.

"Are you well, Miss Natalie?" the girl asked anxiously.

Natalie forced a smile, and then discovered she could not stop smiling. "Yes. Yes, I am very well, thank you. Just a little tired, I think."

And then Richard was there, as tall and sardonic as ever. "May I take you for an ice?" he said incongruously.

She stood without a word and walked beside him across the rose garden to the awning where tea and ices and various sweet and savory snacks could be bought. They found a table, where Richard propped his walking stick and held a chair for her to sit. He took the chair opposite, and they ordered tea and ices from the waitress.

Richard leaned back in his chair, stretching out his bad leg in a pleased, relaxed kind of way that she almost resented. She took a deep breath to bring up the subject of the marriage lines.

"I'm thinking of buying a livery stable in town," he said.

She blinked. "Why would you wish to own such a thing?"

"Oh, lots of reasons. I was a cavalry officer for ten years. If I know anything, I know about horses. And then, I could employ old soldiers to work there and even to run it."

"*Your* old soldiers," she guessed.

"I might also breed horses on my land."

Her heart sank. "You have a large estate?"

"Lord, no. Very much a younger son's portion, but it's a pleasant place and has room for another venture."

"Won't you need to make a big investment in such a project?" she asked. "I suppose your father, the marquess, would help."

"He might," Richard said dubiously. "But I have no intention of asking him. I have a decent amount of prize money that I haven't touched. That will start me off. And I have made up my mind to sell my commission."

"Is that not a very sudden decision?" she asked.

He shrugged. "I will never go back to the army. I know that. I just needed something to take its place as my… *raison d'être*, if you like."

"Horses and a small livery stable?" she said dubiously.

He smiled at her, and she felt her breath vanish. "Among other things. I have stopped—marking time."

She frowned, catching some deeper meaning from his words. He was beginning to live again.

Their tea and ices arrived at their table, and their talk fell to less personal matters. And to the more serious business of appreciating the flavored ices. Although Richard smiled as he ate his, his gaze was constantly on her lips, flooding her with delicious memory as well as the pleasure of the present.

As a group of manufactory girls giggled their way to the large table next to them, she and Richard stood and walked across the gardens to the back gate that led eventually to her cottage. Despite her awareness of him at her side, they did not talk much. Worry about the marriage lines had faded as music soared insistently in her mind, the same melody that had been hovering for days. Only now it was building, and she had to play it, write it *now* before she even looked at the symphony again.

And yet she didn't want Richard to go.

"I need to play," she said in a rush as he opened the door for her.

"May I stay and make plans of my own? Or will my presence annoy you?"

"Of course, you will not annoy me," she said, perhaps too fervently, but she could not hide her pleasure in his request.

She dropped her bundle in the bedchamber from habit, all but tore off her hat, and threw herself down at the pianoforte. She played the insistent tune as far as it would go in her head and dementedly wrote it all down, before turning to the harp to give it breadth and harmony and the counter melody that gave it such power in her mind. She liked it. It seemed to come from deep within her and it *moved* her.

At various times, she was aware of Richard, sitting in the armchair, one ankle crossed over the other knee to hold a notebook steady while he scribbled in it, or tapped his pencil thoughtfully against his teeth. Once, he crossed behind her and went outside and she could hear the low rumble of his voice as he spoke to his old soldiers. And even through her determination to capture every note and nuance from her head to the paper, she found peculiar contentment. As though they were an old married couple, working away at their own tasks in the pleasant knowledge of the other's familiar presence.

And yet this was not a companionship she could ever know. Even if by some miracle Richard loved her as she loved him, he was a marquess's son. Even before her fall to the status of paid itinerant musician, traveling unchaperoned in questionable company, she would have been a poor match for him. Now…

A cup of tea appeared in front of her, and she looked up, bemused, into the scarred face of the man she loved. She smiled, and he dropped a kiss on her lips. Involuntarily, her hand came up to touch his cheek.

"Don't let me disturb you," he said.

She rubbed her forearm across her forehead in a gesture of tiredness. "I… I think I'm finished for the day."

"What is that you were playing? Part of your symphony?"

"No, it doesn't seem to fit there. It is too much to be a song. Maybe it will be a concerto, or… It seems to create itself, so I'll just wait and see." She sipped her tea and watched him bring his over from the hearth. He leaned his hip against the table and drank. He didn't like tea, she recalled, and yet he shared the ritual with her.

"Have you made your plans?" she asked.

"As far as I can for now. I will show you them, soon."

She took another mouthful of tea. "What is wrong with now?"

"I have other plans for now, if you are prepared to indulge me."

Her cup rattled in its saucer as she laid it down too clumsily, for there was a glint of wicked mischief in his eyes.

"Indulge you?" she repeated breathlessly.

"I would like to indulge you, too. In a little afternoon pleasure. If you wish."

Heat flooded her face, paralyzed her tongue and, it seemed, the rest of her body. She could only gaze, helplessly as the smile played around his suddenly sinful lips.

With a last mouthful, he set down his cup and saucer on the table and stretched out one hand to her, drawing her to her feet until her hips came to rest against his and her whole body thrilled to his arousal.

"Will you make love with me, Natalie Derwent?" he murmured in her ear. "Before I explode with desire for you?"

"It's the middle of the afternoon," she managed by way of weak protest.

"The best time," he assured her. "The door is locked, and we are safe. And I want you very, very badly."

She could feel that he did, but his mouth took hers as though to leave no room for doubt. Remembering the men outside, she drew back and went to close the window. After which, she took his hand and led him to the bedchamber.

She had thought there could be no pleasure greater than that he had given her last night, but in her bed that afternoon, with the sun shining through the curtains, and the birds singing their hearts out in the surrounding trees, he showed her there were more and greater joys to be derived from each other's bodies. With his fingers, with his mouth, and his whole being, he gave her pleasure after pleasure until she thought she could not bear it, and then he gave her more.

Panting, almost mindless with bliss, she still knew that the greatest wonder of all was the joy she gave to him. Only that made her weep. Twice. Until he fell asleep kissing the tears from her cheeks.

MONCK RAISED THE glass set in front of him to Davenport.

"Captain Gorse still appears to be at Renwick's Hotel," Davenport said after returning the salute. "He hasn't been back to his Albany rooms in days, and he hasn't been seen at Sedgemoor House either."

"And my lady wife?"

"Played her usual afternoon concert in the pleasure gardens," Davenport said apologetically. "I didn't go myself, but I sent my man."

Damnation. Both her employer and her heroic lover or suitor or whatever he was should have abandoned her flat by now. Moreover, there should have been rumors all around town, ridiculing the pair of them and causing scandalized hands to fly up in delighted horror at the thought of such a woman as Natalie Derwent getting her disreputable paws on such a noble paragon as Lord Richard Gorse.

None of this had materialized.

"Gorse is still protecting her," he said, annoyed.

"Looks like it," Davenport agreed. He shook his head. "Isn't right, though, keeping your wife from you. Not when you're prepared to take her back."

Monck wasn't just prepared to take her back. He *needed* her back. His charms were no longer working, even on Amy Laurel, the silly little songbird at Maida Gardens, and he had run out of money. He had won a bit by judicious cheating at cards, enough to play his part among the town swells and pay an accomplice to help him break into Natalie's cottage.

Mind you, Monck hadn't had to pay his fellow house breaker yet. The man hadn't come near him again, and he wondered if he might risk returning to that tavern. The Bird in Hand. Because clearly desperate measures were called for. He could not pay his tailor. He was dependent on Davenport and a couple of others to buy him dinner and wine, but sooner or later they were going to notice that he never took his turn. Lord Calton already avoided him, though he had been amiable enough to start with.

Fortunately, by means of the same judicious cheating, he had managed to avoid gambling debts which, for some reason, were regarded as debts of honor. He would not yet be run out of town, but card sharping was not his main talent, and it was only a matter of time until he was caught. Before that happened, he needed to regain control of Natalie, flee to the Continent with her, and start her earning her keep in the concert halls if he could.

In between public concerts, there were always the kind of clubs where gentlemen of means appreciated beauty with their music. And Natalie, properly dressed in sheer, low-cut garments, with her icy, touch-me-not attitude, was an irresistible draw. And if the price was right, this time he'd let some wealthy noblemen have her for an hour or two. She owed him for the inconvenience.

And he needed all the money he could get. He no longer felt well, and he needed to rest for the winter, preferably somewhere warm and agreeable and expensive. And Natalie was still his best, if not his only, means of acquiring such means. She had brought in so much before that he had lived off it damned well after she had abandoned him. And they'd live damned well again if only he could get her away from Richard Bloody Gorse.

"Spot of dinner, Monck?" Davenport suggested.

"Why not?" It would be riskier going later to the Bird in Hand, but he expected it was later on that the truly, efficiently bad criminals entered the tavern's hallowed if filthy halls. "Been thinking though, Dav, is that cousin of yours still a magistrate at Bow Street?"

"Temporarily, Monck, temporarily. But yes, he's still there. Why?"

"Because my loving wife might need an additional incentive to see the error of her ways." But first, it was necessary to remove Gorse from his path. Thanks to little Amy, he knew where to find Gorse, and it wasn't Renwick's Hotel.

CHAPTER NINE

"WILL YOU MARRY me, Natalie Derwent?"

The words jerked her back, just as she was drifting off to sleep surrounded by the warmth and weight of his limbs and a glow of emotional and physical happiness.

Her eyes flew open into his. He really had said those words. For an instant, her joy was so intense it felt almost like pain. And then, like a bucket of cold water, she remembered Gerald. And the marriage lines that Richard must have seen.

With a gasp, she pushed him, dislodging him from his position looming over her, so that she could dive out of the bed.

"Are you mocking me?" she demanded. "Or testing me? Whichever, it is unkind. Unnecessarily unkind."

He lay on his back, utterly naked, gazing up at her not with astonishment but with wariness.

"Why would you think a proposal of marriage was either? Given that I am not Gerald Monck."

Seizing her old dressing gown from the back of the door, she struggled into it to try and recover some dignity. Then she untied the shawl-wrapped bundle on the stool and swiped up the marriage lines, which she flung at him.

"Don't pretend you haven't seen that before. It fell out of your coat pocket this morning."

"I wondered. I was looking for it when I was in town." His

tone was casual. To her, this was disastrous, catastrophic, and he spoke of it as though it were a missing grocery list. "I meant to show it to Ludovic Dunne."

Only anger—she wasn't even sure what drove it—prevented her from crumpling into a ball of grief for her lost dreams that had barely begun, her false beliefs in him…

"Why?" she raged. "The better to send me back to him?"

Richard sat in one easy, practiced motion, slid his legs out of bed, and walked toward her, stark naked.

"I have just loved you to the edge of my sanity if not yours and I have proposed marriage. How is that sending you back to him?"

Dear God, he was beautiful. Naked men were not supposed to be beautiful, were they? But his skin seemed to glow, drawn taut over broad shoulders and narrow hips, long legs, and rippling muscle. Even the asymmetry of his missing arm could not detract from that. In fact, somehow it added to the beauty because it was his, his suffering, his courage, part of what made him the man swaggering so deliberately toward her. The hated document dangled carelessly between his fingers.

She backed into the little dressing table, slid around it until she could fall back against the wall. Yet still, he kept coming and did not stop until his naked body touched hers. A deliberate swish of his hips dislodged her robe, and she had to swallow a gasp of sudden, inconvenient arousal as his naked skin found hers in the opening.

"You didn't tell me about that," she threw at him, with a contemptuous jerk of her head to the document between his fingers. "You did not ask me about it. Instead, you seduce me and offer me marriage, while in possession of a document proving my marriage to another very much alive man? What am I supposed to think?"

The document fluttered to the floor. His hard chest against her breasts made them ache for his caresses, distracting her, though she maintained her glare. Even when she felt his arousal beginning to grow.

"You are meant to trust me," he said softly, and bent his head, brushing his lips across hers. A wave of heat rolled through her body. "As I trust you." His lips moved, teasing the corner of her mouth. The tip of his tongue touched the seam of her lips and she gasped. Which seemed to be all he needed. His mouth took hers in a long, sensual kiss that melted her from the inside out. Only the pressure of his body kept her upright against the wall.

"You are meant to know," he whispered against her lips, "that I would never believe that disgrace of a man over anyone, let alone over you. That I would never hurt you." His mouth sank deeper once more so that she could barely comprehend the wonder of his words. "That I love you."

With a sob, she threw both arms around his neck, pressing her cheek hard to his. He stepped back, drawing her with him so that he could get his arm around her. He lifted her over his hip and brought her back to bed.

"I didn't want to tell you until I had discussed it with Dunne," he said, "and had him confirm my own suspicions—not that it is fake, we take that as certain." He sprawled across the bed and reached out his arm to swipe the document off the floor, then brought it back with him as he settled against the pillows beside her. His shoulder, hip, and leg pressed warmly against hers and physical contentment helped settle the turbulent, emotional relief of his words.

"Look. Does it not seem to you that this is all written in the same hand? Even the signatures, though he has made an effort to make them different. Do you have any of his writing to compare this with?"

She shook her head. "No, I threw away everything associated with him. But that looks very like *my* signature, and that is his. I know he can forge mine, for he has done so before. The rest..." She bent over it more closely and frowned. "He could be disguising it. Even the clergyman's signature... But how we could prove—"

She broke off, snatching up the document. "He has signed Amelia Dart's name as a witness!" In growing triumph, she laughed. "Miss Dart had left us weeks before the date on this!"

"No wonder he didn't want me to take it from him," Richard observed. "He will have used her name to make the document more real to me, judging that you would have spoken of her to me or that I might ask you about her. But he obviously didn't want me actually showing it to you."

"It was never meant to stand up in a court of law," she said slowly, "just scare you away from me. So that I have nowhere to turn. He means that I should either share what I have with him or lose everything with what is left of my reputation."

The day had seen tides of emotions, sweeping her up and dropping her back down. This last, downward slide from such a great height closed up her throat. "Richard, even if I am free to do so, I cannot marry you. I am too far beneath you in rank."

"You are a lady of good family. Landed gentry is not despised by anyone."

"My family is decent. *I* am not. I let Gerald change my plans to make myself a superior music teacher and became instead a stage performer, traveling with him in the last weeks without even a chaperone. That can *always* come out, even if by some chance no one connects me with the harpist at Maida Gardens! I am not a fit wife for you."

His hand came up to stroke her head, to settle at her nape. "You are the only wife for me. I am hoping to be the only husband for you. The rest is…noise. I have a powerful family and, somehow, I have made good friends. They will overcome any talk so that it never touches you."

"Richard, your powerful family will hate me!"

"Like Dominic and Viola?"

"Lord and Lady Dominic are different, and you know it. The Marquess of Sedgemoor will not welcome me into his family."

"Actually, I think he will. Though since we are being honest with each other and laying all our cards on the table, I won't pretend it will be so easy. My father is a stubborn and frequently pompous old martinet, but he has one disadvantage."

"What?" she asked dubiously.

"He loves his children. Oh, he tries not to, and seldom allows his failing to show, but he moves heaven and earth to keep us safe. Dominic was mad to follow me into the army, but my father would not risk him. He turned the whole world upside down, to do what he thought was the right thing and keep Dom safe when he was charged with murder. He did the same for me, exerting his influence to keep me out of battle. I got around that, but I was still touched that he tried. And he is very much behind the careers of my other brothers. I used to think it was just his need to control us all, but it isn't. He loves us."

"Then he will want a better wife for you."

He kissed her temple. "It may take time to show him I will only settle for the best. You. But it will happen. Not that it matters. Life may be more comfortable with his blessing, but we do not need it. Do you want to dine in the cottage tonight?"

She did, very much, and so together they prepared a simple meal and shared it with the men, all eating together, al fresco, in the small back garden. The men made her laugh with tales of their captain getting into trouble and getting them out of it, stories of heroism and humor and the everyday life of soldiers.

Then, as the light began to fade, two of the men went off "on patrol" and Richard fetched her shawl and walked with her up to the hotel.

Am I then to have everything? she asked herself with awe. *This wonderful man, love, marriage, respectability?* It had never seemed possible, yet he swung along beside her now in companionable silence, his arm, his hip occasionally brushing against her. This, she thought, was pure happiness.

IT WENT AGAINST the grain to leave Natalie to sleep alone. The sense of peace she gave him, as well as the sheer *rightness* of lying by her side all night, called to him, tempted him. He could be considerate enough to let her body rest. He just wanted to hold her, lie in her embrace.

But his instincts were tingling in an ominous kind of way. So much so that, when he had walked back to the cottage, he sent Daniels to keep watch at the hotel and warned everyone to be extra vigilant. And then he went to bed, with a dagger under the pillow and his sword stick lying beside him.

By now, through his various contacts who obviously included some in polite society, Monck would guess that his fake marriage lines had not repelled Richard. He could well be desperate enough to abduct Natalie by force, even involving decent acquaintances like Calton, who was generally ripe for any mischief, and the other fellow who had been with him at Dominic and Viola's house. And Richard wanted to be ready for him. He could not wait to catch the rat red-handed and have him transported for housebreaking and assault and any other crime they could throw at him. None of it would make up for what he had put Natalie through, for the fear and isolation she had endured because of him.

But Richard would make it as right as he could. On that, he was more determined than anything in all his rather determined life.

Natalie. He wondered if she had been his love at first sight or at first sound. The thought made him smile as he slipped into slumber.

He woke disoriented in darkness, thinking he was in some camp or barracks back in Spain. He wasn't, but why should he imagine... Because fresh air ruffled his hair. Because there was another presence in the room, other breath, other movement.

Every nerve prickled in alarm. He snatched at the sword stick beside him and threw himself upright and away from that breath, just as an arm stabbed viciously downward. Richard swung the stick in the direction of the blacker figure on the other side of the bed and connected with bone and flesh, hard enough to make his assailant grunt.

Like a shadow, the man leapt back from the bed, and Richard threw himself off the other side, shaking the cover from his sword stick. He staggered slightly on his weak leg and was only just in time to parry the lightning-quick lunge of his attacker.

"Smithy!" he yelled to his old sergeant as sparks flew from the two blades clashing in the darkness.

Richard's attacker swore and suddenly changed tack, trying to disengage and bolt from whatever reinforcements he imagined were about to charge to Richard's rescue. Richard lunged toward the open bedchamber door to stop him, but a sudden light blinded him and for his own safety, he had to leap back again.

So, he saw, peering through his narrowed eyes, did his assailant, who had flung up one arm over his eyes while holding his knife before him in protection.

A pistol mechanism clicked, and everyone froze. By the light of the lantern held in Fellows's hand, Smith held the pistol to the intruder's temple.

"Not a twitch," he said severely. "Or I'll be forced to scatter your brains all over a lady's boudoir."

"Lady?" the intruder exclaimed. He dropped his arm from his eyes and stared at Richard. "If that's a lady, I'm the Queen of Sheba."

"That is Captain Gorse," Smith said with dignity.

"And you," Richard added, retrieving the scabbard for his swordstick, "have a good deal of explaining to do."

"Is that pistol loaded?" the man asked nervously.

"No point holding a weapon that isn't," Richard said. "Ask any old soldier. Let us repair to the sitting room."

The intruder seemed game enough to do so, especially when Smith moved the pistol back from his head. However, encountering Havers in the sitting room with another pistol, his shoulders slumped.

Richard set about lighting lamps and candles so that they could see their enemy. Naturally, it was not Monck himself, but an unexpectedly small, wiry man with cold, hard eyes and a furtive expression.

Smith pushed him onto the wooden chair. "Hands on your head where I can see them."

The would-be assassin sighed and obeyed.

Richard blew out the spill and dropped it in the grate. "You were expecting a man."

"Beg pardon, cap'n?"

"You were surprised to hear the bedchamber belonged to a lady," Richard reminded him.

"Well, no sign of a lady in there," the man said reasonably.

"Allow me to clarify. You were sent to attack a man."

"Don't hold with attacking females."

"What's your name?" Richard asked.

"Smith."

Sergeant Smith poked him with the butt of his pistol. "That's my name. Try again."

"Jones."

"It will do for now," Richard said peaceably when Smith seemed inclined to backhand their captive for cheek. "And the man who sent you?"

"Who says anyone sent me?"

"I do," Richard replied. "There are bigger houses to burgle just over the hill and a large, expensive hotel within walking distance. No one comes of their own accord to murder a stranger in a small cottage with nothing worth stealing."

"Nice sword-stick," Jones said. "And I'll bet you've some rolls of soft lying around, a decent tie pin, sleeve buttons."

"You're prepared to hang for sleeve buttons and a plain tie pin? And an easily identifiable sword stick?"

Jones's gaze flickered to the front door, where Havers lounged, his pistol resting across one arm. "What do you want, cap'n?"

"The name of the man who sent you."

"And then what would I get?"

"You might not get killed breaking into a lady's cottage and trying to murder an officer and a gentleman," Smith retorted.

"To say nothing of him being a marquess's son," Fellows added. "Quite the nob is our captain. An actual lord."

Jones swore beneath his breath. "Seems to me we've both been set up. Was a nob that sent me. At least he sounded like one, though he knows too much thieves' cant if you ask me."

"Did he give you his name?"

"I insisted. Especially as he only paid me half up front. I'm to get the rest once he knows you're dead."

Richard's lips quirked. "Sadly, you will be sacrificing that."

"Very glad to," Jones assured him, not entirely convincingly. "Nob was called Monck."

"And you would testify to that?"

"Testify?" Jones said uneasily. "No one'll believe a word *I* say. And no telling but the magistrate will know me anyway and then I'll swing."

"You are rather caught between the devil and the deep, blue sea," Richard mused. "You don't appear to have any good options left."

"No." Jones looked genuinely lugubrious.

"I will make you this offer," Richard said, easing onto the other chair. "I will take you not to a magistrate but to a lawyer, who will write down your testimony and you will sign or make your mark, which will be duly witnessed. This will involve using your real name, and it had better be provable. If it is, and everything goes well, it might be possible to lose you between the lawyer's office and Bow Street. But if we do this, you had better find an alternative career, my friend, because if I ever come across you furthering that of an assassin, I will kill you myself."

For once, Jones seemed to have nothing to say. He gazed at Richard, who let all his lethal rage into his eyes, then smiled with all the ice that had formed around his heart before Natalie.

Jones swallowed. "Understood, cap'n. I'll do it your way. I'll even spread the word you and your men here ain't to be touched." He brightened. "Unless you'd like me to kill Monck for you?"

Tempting. Damned tempting. But... "That won't be necessary. If he dies this year, it will be by the rope or by my hand. Just do as I've asked."

"Deal." Jones stretched out one hand from his head until Smith leveled his pistol, when he quickly stuck it back on his head again.

CHAPTER TEN

THE FOLLOWING MORNING, Natalie found Daniels waiting for her outside the hotel.

"Morning, miss," he said cheerfully. "Back to the cottage?"

"Indeed."

"Catain left this for you." He produced a slightly battered note, folded twice, from inside his coat and passed it to her.

Her heart sank. He had gone off somewhere again without her, and she was hungry just for a sight of him. Though she wanted to stuff the note in her reticule and read it in privacy, it seemed she could not wait. Moving out of the way of an arriving carriage, she unfolded the note and read it quickly.

We had a bit of excitement here last night, which I believe has helped our cause. I've taken Smith with me into town, so I may not be back in time for your concert this afternoon. However, I hope to bring you good news later today. Please keep your escort at all times. Yours, R.

Hardly the letter of a devoted lover, she thought anxiously. Only then she realized that was exactly what it was. He was looking after her, protecting her, helping her, and she could never want for more. Besides which, he was being discreet, using no names and declaring no improper affection. At least he had called himself hers.

She stuffed the note into her reticule and, keeping to their custom, walked ahead of Daniels, taking the shortcut through the pleasure gardens and out through the top gate to the track. Only then, seeing no one around, did she turn to Daniels.

"What happened last night?"

"Someone broke into the cottage. The captain and the others caught him, put the fear of God into him, and took him into town."

"To Bow Street?"

"Presume so, but I don't know. Only had a quick word with Havers when he brought me that."

"And he… No one is hurt?"

"'Course not," Daniels scoffed.

"Did Monck send this man?" she asked bluntly.

Daniels shrugged. "I suppose so, but you'll have to ask the captain. Hopefully, he won't be too long. What do you plan to do this morning?"

"Music," she said with a distracted smile. In the absence of Richard, she would devote herself to the new piece that was all about him and her feelings for him. She had come to realize that yesterday as they were making love and the music had followed her, soaring into climax.

At the cottage, she wormed some more details about last night's disturbance from the men, including the heart-stopping fact that if the captain hadn't moved quickly, he'd have been dead in her bed. And the guilty assurance that the housebreaker had managed to break in through the front door during the only five minutes there had been no one guarding that side of the house. By the time the captain had yelled Smith's name, the sergeant had already discovered the open front door and summoned the others.

After such hair-raising confidences, Natalie found it *necessary* to lose herself in music. So she did, leaving the men to catch up on sleep as best they could in the little camps they had set up in and around the cottage grounds.

Working, she lost track of time and had to rush to change for the midday concert. Just as she reached for her shawl, a loud, peremptory knock at the door made her jump. Dropping the shawl around her shoulders, she went to the door and opened it.

Two strange men stood there, both in red waistcoats, though why such a detail should strike her she had no idea. They didn't remove their hats.

"Miss Natalie Derwent?" one said.

"Yes." She glanced beyond them and was relieved to see Richard's men scowling on either side of her visitors, only feet away from them.

"We're from the magistrate's office at Bow Street and—"

"Oh, good!" she exclaimed. "What news do you have for me?"

The strangers looked slightly baffled at this. "Bad news," one said dryly. "We're arresting you on suspicion of murder. You have to come with us."

Her mouth fell open. *Murder?*

"Murder of who?" Daniels asked scathingly. "The lady won't even stand on a spider."

Blood was singing in her ears. These men were Bow Street Runners.

"That's what you think," one runner said pityingly to Daniels. "This one killed her own mother."

AFTER THE INITIAL difficulty of establishing Jones's real name, which turned out to be Obadiah Hindmarsh, the business of recording his testimony against Monck went well enough. And his statement was duly witnessed by Smith and by Dunne's clerk.

"You should still have him charged with attempted murder and house-breaking," Dunne said austerely as Smith escorted the would-be assassin from the premises.

Richard sighed. "I know, but if Smith loses him between here and Bow Street, there's not much I can do."

"You could go with them."

"I could. But then I wouldn't hear about the rest of this evidence you've been collecting. Come on, Dunne, let's have it."

Dunne tapped his fingers on the supposed marriage lines that he had been looking at. "Miss Derwent is quite correct. The governess, Miss Dart, had left Italy by the time she is meant to have witnessed this marriage. I know this because I spoke to her yesterday afternoon."

Richard's eyebrows flew up. "She is in London? Miss Derwent will want to know that."

"I understand Miss Dart has also been anxious about Miss Derwent, and she was very sorry to hear about the mother's death. Her testimony would be useful in showing Monck's manipulation of the Derwent ladies—she was on to him long before they were. Miss Derwent was by no means his only female interest. In fact, he used Miss Derwent's money, earned from her concerts, to buy presents for his—ah—inamoratas. Miss Dart knew he was stealing and confronted him. He then told Mrs. Derwent that the governess was pursuing him romantically, and the old lady sent her packing. Though she suspects Monck himself forged the written dismissal denying her most of the salary she was due."

Richard swore beneath his breath.

"Then there is the physician," Dunne said.

"Physician?"

"The Scottish physician who treated Mrs. Derwent in her last illness. His name is Dr. Swinton. He is living in Hampstead now, and he has some interesting information. He suspected Mrs. Derwent was poisoned."

"*Poisoned?* Dear God…"

"As you say. He passed his suspicions on to the authorities when the lady died, but justice apparently moves slowly. By the time anything was done about it, Miss Derwent and Monck had moved on."

"And he was in sole charge of her," Richard said grimly. "Or thought he was."

"Worried for her, the doctor did track her to Rome, where he heard she was playing at the kind of halls to which a gentleman does not take his wife or his sister. But he could not find her. They had probably moved on again, or she had already left him."

"The more I hear of this snake," Richard said with quiet savagery, "the more I wish I'd finished him when he gave me that piece of rubbish."

"And then I would be defending you at your murder trial instead of pursuing Monck. And I suspect you have rather more to live for."

Richard couldn't help the smile tugging at his lips. "I do."

Dunne opened his mouth to reply, but a sudden commotion from the outer office made him frown instead.

"I'm sorry, you will have to wait!" came the sound of the clerk's raised voice, swiftly followed by thuds very like marching feet and, "You cannot go in there!"

The door burst open to reveal Daniels, Havers, Fellows, and Smith, whom they must have picked up in the street after he had "lost" Jones, born Obadiah Hindmarsh.

"Sir, I am sorry," the clerk began furiously from behind them.

"I think you must let them in," Richard said, a sense of foreboding twisting his gut. "What has happened?"

"Bow Street Runners came for Miss Natalie," Daniels blurted.

"*What?*" Richard surged to his feet without the aid of either his stick or Dunne's desk.

"They're charging her with murder. Of her mother, for God's sake."

"Tell me you didn't let them take her," Richard uttered, though he already knew from the way they had burst in that they had. "Idiots! They weren't runners, they didn't take her anywhere near Bow Street. They've handed her straight to—"

"They did," Daniels interrupted.

"Richard blinked. "What?"

"They did take her to the Bow Street magistrate's house. We followed her. They really were runners."

"That is insane." Richard dragged his hand through his hair, then reached blindly for his walking stick. "I have to go there."

"No," Dunne said, busily writing. "If we can, we need to nip this in the bud, or she could await trial in prison. Which is as likely to kill her as not. I will go to Bow Street and see what can be done. You, my lord, and your men have other equally important tasks."

⇶✕⇷

As though trapped in a nightmare, Natalie suffered the journey to town with the two Bow Street runners, who regarded her with utter contempt.

"My mother died more than two years ago," she said to them. "How am I charged with this now? And in England! My mother died in Italy."

"Which is where you'll be going to stand trial I expect," one of the runners said loftily. "If they have trials there."

"That makes no sense," she said confused. "Who has charged me with such a horrible crime?"

"Horrible is right. Some big wig foreign gent—a count or a marquess or something—has come for you. You'll be handed over to him all legal-like."

She stared at him wildly. "None of this makes any sense," she repeated.

"Neither does doing in your old mum," the quieter runner said austerely.

"Exactly! Of course, I never did such a thing."

"Save it," she was advised, "for the magistrate."

Had her mother been murdered? She had to force herself to go back over those awful days of Mama's final illness and death, before Gerald had hurried her away when she wasn't yet ready to leave her mother's grave. Life had been a numbing nightmare of grief and loss and loneliness, punctuated by concerts in places she had known were not respectable. She hadn't cared at the time because music had been her only solace.

But Mama had been dead by then. She remembered the doctor, Doctor Swinton, who had been traveling to gain knowledge of medicine in other countries. He had been gravely worried about Mama, and rightly so. She had been so distressingly ill.

Once, she had come upon Dr. Swinton sniffing at the glass in which Natalie had served her mother the medicine he had prescribed.

Dear God, did he suspect me? Has it taken all this time for him to send authorities after me? How could he even imagine *I would do such a thing?*

Would she find him in Bow Street with the magistrate, along with this Italian nobleman who had come to take her back? Would the men be able to get word to Richard in time? She could not bear to be whisked away to another country without him even knowing.

Her mind whirled and panicked, but nothing made any sense to her except that this was a terrible dream from which she would eventually awaken, perhaps even to find Richard right beside her...

But she did not waken. The nightmare went on into the magistrate's house, where a new fear hit her that she would be put in a prison cell. Though she would have to get used to that reality if this went on, if she could not prove her innocence.

How can I prove I did not kill my own mother?

And then, *How can they prove I did, when I did nothing but care for her?*

The last thought brightened her enough to restore at least some of her dignity as she was dragged past a long line of sad and furtive people, some clearly drunk, some gaudy, including several obvious women of the night, pathetically young and garishly painted.

"'Ere, why's she skipping the queue?" someone demanded. "What's she done that's more important than what I done?"

That got a laugh, but Natalie's captors ignored all comments, merely dragged her along to the front, where they exchanged words with another man by a door. And there they waited until the door opened and a sheepish-looking man strode out and slunk past the line of waiting prisoners.

The doorman jerked his head, and the runners hauled Natalie inside with unnecessary force.

A youngish man with an alarmingly sweaty head and a clerk writing busily beside him, said, "Well, well, who have we here?"

"One Natalie Derwent, sir, accused of murder. Matricide," said the runner, pronouncing the last word with peculiar relish.

Natalie shuddered.

"Ah, yes, the marchese's prisoner," the magistrate said jovially. "Best fetch him in. Now then, young woman, state your name for the record if you please."

"Natalie Derwent. Sir, please tell me what is happening? Why I have been brought here?"

"Just a formality to bind you over to the authority of the marchese," the magistrate said in what he might have imagined were reassuring tones.

"What marchese could possibly have authority over me, let alone over you?"

"There is no authority here over *me*," he said irritably, "or over the laws of England. It is a matter of cooperation and facing punishment where your crimes were committed."

"Sir, I committed no crime," she insisted.

"Then it will be for the courts in Rome or wherever to establish that. Today, we will hear only the charges against you and give you over to the custody of the marchese and his men. And here is his excellency."

Almost bemused, Natalie watched a dark, foreign-looking gentleman strut into the court between two hulking great fellows. He wore lace at his throat and cuffs, and his over-long black curls looked like a stage villain's wig. He even wore luxurious mustaches. More than that she did not see, for she was distracted by the magistrate's demand for the marchese's name.

"Il Marchese del Pietrodusa," the newcomer pronounced.

"And for what crimes is this woman, Natalie Derwent, wanted in your country?"

"For murder, signor. The murder of her own mother by poison in the year of our Lord eighteen hundred and seventeen, during the month of April. You have the details before you."

"I do," the magistrate said so hastily that Natalie suspected the details were in Italian and he could not even read them.

Natalie, wrestling with the bizarre idea that she had heard the marchese's voice before, tried to concentrate on more than the injustice of these proceedings.

"I need someone who knows the law to speak for me," she insisted. "I cannot be handed over to this stranger only on his say so, on some trumped-up charge that is not only wrong but vile and insulting and iniquitous."

"I know the law, young woman," said the magistrate. "What would you like me to explain to you?"

The words burst from her, no doubt unwisely. "That in the absence of any evidence to support his silly, cruel accusations, I am free to go!"

"The honored magistrate has the evidence before him," the marchese said haughtily.

"A piece of paper," she raged. "It is not enough, and I want my own solicitor!"

"Perhaps I shall do, ma'am?" said quite another voice. A tall man with pale blond hair sauntered down the room as though it belonged to him.

Natalie stared. "Mr. Dunne! You could not be more welcome! I am being accused of murdering my own mother in Italy, and this magistrate is trying to give me into the custody of this marchese, to stand trial in Italy. I have not even seen the evidence against me!"

The magistrate waved his paper around as he glared at Mr. Dunne. "And you are, sir?"

"Ludovic Dunne, at your service."

The magistrate looked momentarily alarmed, and it came to Natalie that he was cutting legal corners for a friend. In which case, a professional lawyer of Mr. Dunne's high reputation was the last person he would want opposing him.

"I don't believe we've had the pleasure," Mr. Dunne remarked.

"My name is Budd," the magistrate said with dignity. "Sir John Budd, temporarily standing in as Bow Street magistrate."

"Sir John." Mr. Dunne bowed again to the magistrate as he came to stand beside Natalie. "I believe I came upon a cousin of yours recently. Davenport, was it?"

And just like that, perhaps because of Dunne's mention of the name, or because she was staring in weird fascination at the Italian, she recognized the marchese.

She should have known him at once. If she had not been so frightened and overwhelmed, she would have seen straight through his disguise.

"Very likely," Budd said hurriedly, so hurriedly that she knew he was indeed cutting corners and to please his cousin Davenport, the friend of Gerald Monck.

Damn Gerald all over again. He had found a way to manipulate the law to regain control over her. Only none of this was remotely legal. She swung around to Mr. Dunne to tell him exactly what was going on, but he only smiled at her reassuringly.

"The point is," the magistrate pursued with dignity, "I am perfectly satisfied with the marchese's credentials and the strength of his case against this young woman."

"Are you?" Ludovic Dunne turned an amused gaze on the marchese, who seemed to be trying quite hard to keep his back to him while still looking respectfully toward the magistrate. "While I find it very strange that a nobleman of such rank should interest himself in the fetching and transporting of felons. Perhaps I may see these credentials and this evidence?"

Budd looked as if he would refuse, but without instruction, the clerk suddenly bobbed out of his seat, snatched up the paper, and bore it across the floor to Mr. Dunne.

"Thank you," Dunne said, stretching the paper toward Natalie so that they could both read it.

"It is in Italian," the magistrate said with dignity.

"As it happens, I speak a little of the language," Mr. Dunne said. He smiled. "As does Miss Derwent. If we struggle with understanding any of it, I'm sure the marchese will help."

Natalie spared Dunne a glance of mingled indignation and awe. Was he *baiting* "the marchese"? She still felt too much at the mercy of this charade to risk alienating anyone. She forced her attention back to the Italian document.

An impressive seal took up a large corner of the document, although it was just smudged enough to make the wording impossible to read. The letter purported to be from a court of law in a town she had never heard of, introducing the most noble Marquese del Pietrodusa and empowering him to bring back the suspect Natalie Derwent for questioning and trial in the matter of the murder of her mother, Mrs. Louisa Derwent in 1817, with the kind cooperation of the law authorities in England.

"Two oddities strike me immediately," Dunne observed. "The first being, this is not how legal matters are normally handled. The second being the writing of this...document." Leaving Natalie holding the missive, he bent and rummaged in his document case and came up with another document, which he held beside the other. It was her supposed marriage lines. And the writing was remarkably similar.

He took the marchese's document from her and walked toward the window, holding it up to the light and then he walked across to the magistrate's desk and plonked both papers down between the clerk and the magistrate.

"Perhaps the marchese would care to explain why his letter

from the court is written in the same hand as a certificate of marriage? Perhaps the priest handles matters of law in… whichever town this purports to come from, because I see no sign of that either."

Gerald, in the marchese's theatrical voice, said with dignity, "Many people in official life have been taught the same hand in the same schools. Similarities are inevitable."

"I expect it is also inevitable that they use exactly the same paper, watermarked as you will see by the name of its maker. Based in Hertfordshire." Mr. Dunne let that sink in for a little. There was absolute silence in the room. "I'm sure you will agree, Sir John, that if one of those documents is a forgery, the other is also."

"Not necessarily," the magistrate said weakly. "One could surely have been copied from the other. But I'm sure the matter is academic. Paper manufactured in England could easily turn up in Italy."

"True, though this particular company sells solely to the British market. Be that as it may, the supposed marriage lines are most definitely forged. This lady, a Miss Dart, who apparently signed as a witness, was in London on the date of this supposed marriage."

"Do you have proof of that?" Gerald spluttered, "the marchese" slipping slightly in his anger or panic or both.

"Of course, I do," Dunne replied. "I am extremely fastidious about evidence. Perhaps *the marchese* would like to see for himself?"

The marchese, clearly, did not want to go anywhere near him. He took a couple of steps toward the desk and paused, trying to look haughty, as though waiting for the documents to be brought to his noble person. The obliging clerk began to rise once more, but Ludovic Dunne was faster, whipping the documents off the desk and advancing on "the marchese" so quickly that the gentleman actually took a step backward and threw out his hands to ward Dunne off.

But Natalie understood Dunne's next move. It was time to expose the marchese, and nothing would give her greater pleasure. With all eyes on Dunne and "the marchese," it was easy to shift away from the runners, who had been watching proceedings with their jaws dropping, and take a couple of paces forward.

Dunne held the documents out in one hand, but "the marchese," clearly wary, reached out to snatch them with his left. Natalie jumped and grabbed the wig from "the marchese's" head. His free hand flew up too late to save it, and Dunne used the moment to jerk up his hand and yank the elegant mustaches from the imposter's upper lip.

The magistrate was on his feet, the runners advancing, though with no clear purpose. The "marchese's" supposed guards were backing quietly toward the door.

"What the devil do you mean by assaulting a gentleman?" Sir John thundered.

"This is no gentleman, sir," Dunne declared. "But one Gerald Monck, born here in London, and once betrothed to the lady he persuaded you to have dragged here, Miss Derwent. He is a fraud and the author of both of those documents. He is, moreover, the suspect sought by certain authorities in Italy for the poisoning of Mrs. Louisa Derwent."

His eyes flickered to Natalie, who stood frozen, staring at him, the wig still clutched in her no longer triumphant fingers. "I'm sorry," he murmured. "There was no time to—"

The door burst open again to a lot of shouting and running of feet. A sob escaped Natalie's lips, for it was Richard who strode in, his walking stick clicking purposefully on the floor to make sure he out-sped everyone else. Behind him came a gaggle of his men surrounding a man and a woman. And closely following were several outraged officials and guards and even some of the rabble waiting to appear before the magistrate.

"What is the meaning of this?" Sir John shouted, springing to his feet, his voice high with sudden fear. "Clear my rooms immediately! I am in the midst of a most difficult case! And, Mr.

Dunne, if you have no more proof than a gentleman's vanity—"

"I do, sir," Dunne replied, his pleasant voice carrying easily over the hubbub in the room. "My proof has just walked in with Captain Lord Richard Gorse, whom you may already know? Certainly, he is slightly acquainted with your cousin, Mr. Davenport. Lord Richard, will you tell Sir John the name of this man?"

"Gerald Monck," Richard said grimly, stalking straight over to Natalie and grasping her hand. "He was once betrothed to Miss Derwent and has been trying to convince me that she is, in fact, married to him."

"Thank you, my lord," Dunne said, already turning away from him. "Miss Dart?"

Natalie let out a gasp, trying to peer through the throng of people.

"My thanks for your prompt arrival," Dunne said politely. "Do *you* know this man?"

The woman who had entered among Richard's men stepped free of her escort. It really was her old friend and governess, Amelia Dart.

"Gerald Monck," Amelia said clearly. "When I was employed as governess and companion to the family and traveled with them in Italy, I watched him lie and steal from both Mrs. and Miss Derwent for many weeks before he had me dismissed. He and Miss Derwent were once betrothed, thought they were not married when I saw them last in February 1817."

"Your honor!" Gerald cried, outraged. "We are not here to debate my identity!"

"Oh, I think we are," Dunne said harshly, and the whole room quietened. Sir John sat down again with a thud. "Amongst other services to humanity, Doctor Swinton, you were the physician who treated Mrs. Derwent in Italy?"

The dignified young gentleman stood beside Miss Dart, reminding Natalie unbearably of the worst times of her life, and yet the sight of him was so blessedly welcome. "I was. I believed she was being poisoned and so informed the authorities. After the lady died, they established who bought the poison and from whom. Monck bought it and laced it into her food and drink and later her medicine whenever he could. They are still looking for him."

"Then how can he hope to shift the blame to Miss Derwent?" Sir John demanded, looking both irate and confused.

"He cannot," Richard said contemptuously. "He wants only to cow her into earning money for him, as she did before through her music recitals and the compositions for which he took the credit. In pursuit of which goal, he has made shameless use of your cousin's good nature and your own."

Sir John's mouth opened and closed like that of a landed fish. No sound came out. Gerald was backing toward the door until he bumped into Smith and Daniels, who grinned wolfishly at him, causing him to bolt in the other direction. The runners, who must have managed to follow the bizarre proceedings well enough, stood threateningly in front of him.

Richard began to walk, leading Natalie away as if nothing could prevent him. And she had the odd notion that nothing and no one could.

"I leave Monck to you and the law, Sir John," he said coolly. "With the valedictory message that if he finds any way to come near Miss Derwent again, he may have time—just—to regret it. And now, I am taking Miss Derwent home. Good day."

A cheer went up from the ragged defendants clustered around the door. The magistrate's clerk grinned openly, as did Ludovic Dunne, Dr. Swinton, and Miss Dart. The crowd parted like the Red Sea to allow Natalie and Richard through.

"Good on you, sir!" someone proclaimed.

"You look after the lady, sir! Bloody law…!"

Natalie clung to Richard's arm, hardly able to walk for the trembling of her legs.

CHAPTER ELEVEN

A N HOUR LATER, she sat, dazed and happy, not at home as Richard had promised, but upon a sofa in Lord and Lady Dominic's drawing room. Richard sat very close beside her, still holding her hand. Or it might have been she who clung to his fingers. It no longer seemed to matter which.

Their hostess had served them tea and savory morsels and cakes and listened avidly to their tale of Gerald's gall and the doings at the magistrate's house. Both Lord and Lady Dominic had welcomed their uninvited and even unknown visitors with hospitable good humor.

Natalie had been unable to keep the tears back as she had been reunited with Miss Dart and thanked Dr. Swinton for everything he had done.

"You will think me so stupid," she had sobbed to them both. "I had my suspicions he was behind your dismissal, Amelia, though I was too late to prevent it. I never guessed the depths of his perfidy. It never entered my head that anyone could have killed my mother, let alone that it could have been him to…"

"He hustled you away from the scene of his crime before anyone but I had guessed," Dr. Swinton said grimly. "I tried to find you, but I lost you in Rome."

"I left him in Rome," Natalie said. "I suppose the numbness of grief had begun to wear off by then. But also, his behavior had become too blatant for me to ignore. He had lovers. He had taken all of my money. But I stole back what he had left lying in his room one night and set off for home. I hid from him for two years."

"There will be no more hiding," Richard said firmly, and she could not help dragging his hand to her cheek.

"Thank you," she whispered. "Thank you all. He almost had me delivered into his hands."

"What would you have done if he had got you into his power?" Amelia Dart asked curiously.

"Murdered him probably," Natalie replied with a grimace. "I would certainly have got away from him somehow, for he had nothing left to cow me with, and I have every reason to live my own life. I am no longer the confused, dependent, foolish little girl."

"You never were," Miss Dart informed her. "You were merely trusting, and Monck diabolically plausible."

In spite of everything, Natalie's lips twitched. "He wasn't so plausible today, was he? He was like a stage villain!"

"Plausible enough to fool the magistrate and Davenport," Richard pointed out. "Dunne had the benefit of knowing all about him, as did you, so his masquerade was much simpler for both of you to spot."

The drawing room door opened, and a footman announced, "Lord Sedgemoor, ma'am."

"Oh dear," Lady Dominic said, jumping to her feet just as a tall, distinguished gentleman stalked into the room.

Though beyond middle years, he appeared full of vigor. His shrewd, intelligent eyes, swept around the room, coming to rest at last on Richard. And on his hand joined to Natalie's. Natalie tried to withdraw her fingers, but Richard held on, as he and others rose to greet his father.

"Oh dear, indeed," Lord Sedgemoor said scathingly.

"Only because we have eaten all the cakes," Lady Dominic said smoothly, "and I would rather welcome you more hospitably. Good afternoon, my lord, will you allow me to present my guests?"

The marquess gave a regal inclination of his head.

"Miss Derwent, Miss Dart, and Dr. Swinton. Mr. Dunne, of course, you will remember."

Natalie, at last, retrieved her hand to make her curtsey, and as they all sat down, Richard made no effort to take it back. Over fresh tea, awkward small talk was made, but Miss Dart and the doctor took their leave very shortly afterward, closely followed by Ludovic Dunne.

There was a short silence as the door closed behind Mr. Dunne. The marquess's sons exchanged glances. The marquess smiled faintly and sipped his tea.

Richard said, "I would like you to be the first to know, sir, that Miss Derwent has agreed to marry me."

Had she? Not in so many words, but since she could endure no future without him, she did not dispute his claim.

"Congratulations!" Dominic reached over to thump his brother on the back, while Lady Dominic managed to smile in pleasure and still regard her father-in-law with some wariness.

"*Agreed*, has she?" the marquess said with insulting skepticism. "Perhaps she has not heard, as I have, that you have been running about with some juggler or other strumpet from Maida Gardens."

Richard hauled himself furiously to his feet, but before he could speak, Natalie said, "Then you heard wrongly, my lord. But since your insult is quite blatantly aimed at me rather than my imaginary rival for your son's affections, you must allow me to say in return that I cannot juggle. On the other hand, I have had enough of rude men masquerading as gentlemen to last me a lifetime. I can assure you that I have as little desire for your company as you clearly have for mine. We need not receive each other, though naturally you and Richard, who seems for some reason to want your lordship's blessing, may arrange your meetings to suit yourselves."

In the stunned silence, Natalie raised her almost empty cup

and sipped before returning it to its saucer.

"You deserved every word of that, Papa," Lord Dominic said quietly.

Natalie risked a glance at Richard, who didn't look angry at all anymore. Instead, his eyes were blazing with laughter as they held hers. An involuntary smile tugged at her lips in response. Without taking his gaze from hers, Richard said, "You owe my betrothed an apology, Father. I hope you are gentleman enough to make it."

"Your betrothed is not afraid to stand up for herself," Lord Sedgemoor observed, voice and face unreadable.

"I have had to," Natalie said. "Circumstances have required me to fend for myself, which I have done honestly and honorably. My birth is not noble, but it is gentle. I shall not shame your son. I hope you will say the same."

The marquess blinked once, then let out a bark of what seemed like genuine laughter. "Well, you shoot straight, I'll say that for you."

"And?" Richard pressed.

"And I apologize without reserve for my earlier words," Lord Sedgemoor said. "They were designed to test you but were nevertheless quite unconscionable. I would like to hear your story."

"Before you do so," Richard said, dropping back beside Natalie on the sofa, "Dominic and I also have some things to discuss with you. And with Natalie, actually, since events rather intervened this morning. You suggested Dominic stands for Parliament when Gatting stands down."

"I did."

"I don't want to, sir," Dominic said flatly. "I can do more for my cause of prison reform while remaining outside of Parliament, but with connections to the inside. And my politics are pretty much the opposite of yours."

"As are mine," Richard said, "though I am, by nature, more flexible. I would be willing to stand for Gatting's seat. I would vote with you when my conscience allowed, but against you on everything else. I will listen to you and talk, but I will not be browbeaten or forced."

"As if I would try," Sedgemoor muttered, scowling. "What use to me is an unreliable vote in the Commons?"

Richard blinked. "You thought *Dom's* would be reliable? With respect, Papa, it isn't about what I can do for you, but what I can do for my country. I've done the physical fighting. Now I would like to help make a country that is worthy of the men who sacrificed their lives and limbs for it. And I believe we could help each other toward that goal."

Sedgemoor stared at him. "Pretty speech. But the Palace of Westminster is full of stairs."

"I can manage stairs," Richard said evenly.

"What does your betrothed think?" Sedgemoor flung suddenly at Natalie.

"I think it is a wonderful idea," Natalie said at once, winning an immediate smile from Richard. "You mean to do this, as well as the livery stable and the farming and the horse breeding?"

"I do. The farm is only a day's ride from London. We could go down tomorrow and see it if you like."

"Perhaps not tomorrow."

"No, I should set about procuring a special license," Richard agreed.

"And I should have a conversation with Mr. Renwick. I missed today's midday concert and, besides, I suspect his lordship and I are in agreement that I cannot be your wife and play the harp at Maida Gardens."

"Dashed right we are!" Sedgemoor said fervently.

"I THINK THAT went quite well," Richard said sometime later as they entered Natalie's cottage.

She cast a sardonic glance back over her shoulder. "Introducing me to your father? I'd hate to be part of a situation with him that went badly."

"He liked you," Richard said, closing the door and leaning his back against it. "He'll never speak to you like that again."

"Because he doesn't want to provoke a war with you."

His lips twitched. "It was clever of you to point out the risk—allowing us to make our own arrangements to meet!"

"Actually, I meant it. I won't have someone in my home who does not respect me, and I have no intention of visiting theirs. Though I would never be so cruel as to try and part you."

He smiled and pushed himself off the door. "It will never come to that now. He will be almost as proud of you as I am. There is a layer of steel in you, Natalie Derwent. I like that."

"I think I have just found it again," she said, taking off her bonnet and dropping it on the table.

"I think you found mine, too. I have been…drifting."

She turned, winding her arms around his neck so naturally, that happiness seemed to spread upward from his toes. "You have been *recovering*, Richard. I think we both have. It is…good to do so together."

He held her loosely around the waist. "Then you are content to marry me?"

She touched his cheek, her eyes warm and loving. "Of course I am. If you love me."

"You know I love you. You have always known."

She lifted her face for his kiss, which began as a sweet promise, and somehow lingered and grew into something altogether more sensual. "Somewhere very deep in my heart, perhaps I hoped," she whispered. "I even daydreamed a little… How could you so quickly become as necessary to me as breathing?"

"I don't know, but it binds us both."

Another kiss, longer and deeper, until he was in danger of forgetting the things that had to be said.

He pressed his cheek to hers. "Tell me, am I right to believe that performing is not the heart of music for you, that you will not miss it?"

"I came to hate it with Gerald. Here, it was necessary. I like to move people with my music, but mostly, I like to play."

"Could you be happy only playing informally at society or charity events?"

"Yes," she said at once.

"And you will finish your symphony and compose more and more music that will become wonderfully famous across the world. And of course, your popular songs with Mr. Laurie."

"Under what name shall I compose?" she wondered, untying his cravat. "Bearing in mind women's compositions will always be regarded unheard as second rate."

"N. Derwent," he suggested. "Everyone will presume you are a man."

She kissed his throat. "Or N. Gorse."

His hand shifted up her back, finding and releasing the hooks of her gown, a task that was definitely becoming easier with practice. "I like that even better."

"I think I will enjoy being a political hostess, too, and a country lady, helping with your causes and charities of my own..."

"You will be so busy, I hope you will still have time to make love with your husband."

"I will consider it my first duty," she assured him as he brushed her gown to the floor. She stepped out of it and began to lead him to the bedchamber. "And my first pleasure."

After that, he was surprised they made it to the bed in time, for with shocking impatience, he had to pin her to the nearest wall, to feel all of her against him, and kiss her until they were both dizzy. In the end, dignity and consideration won out over his crazy impulse to take her there against the wall. It was another disadvantage of having only one arm. But somehow, when they fell together onto the bed, none of that mattered, only the love and the joy they brought each other.

And the joy of being together only increased over the next

couple of days until they were married at Sedgemoor House with the marquess's blessing. Amelia Dart attended as her bridesmaid and Lord Dominic stood up with Richard. There followed a surprisingly merry wedding breakfast, probably because most of the Gorses were so relieved that she could speak the King's English and didn't eat with her fingers.

They spent their wedding night at Renwick's Hotel, and in the morning pressed on to Richard's charming little estate which they set about making their chief home.

Later, there was a small house in London, too—a gift from the marquess, along with a beautiful harp that made Natalie forgive him for everything. Richard employed old soldiers, his own men, and many others, in their homes and in the livery stable, and with the horses he began to buy and breed. He made a great impact in Parliament, although he often diverged from his father's wishes.

And Natalie finished her symphony and the piece that was Richard's and played both at a very well-received charity concert.

It was a busy and fulfilling life, full of love and laughter, companionship, and friendship. And happy children. So, although hardly a gentleman of leisure, for the first time in his life, Richard really did feel like a gentleman of pleasure.

About Mary Lancaster

Mary Lancaster lives in Scotland with her husband, three mostly grown-up kids and a small, crazy dog.

Her first literary love was historical fiction, a genre which she relishes mixing up with romance and adventure in her own writing. Her most recent books are light, fun Regency romances written for Dragonblade Publishing: *The Imperial Season* series set at the Congress of Vienna; and the popular *Blackhaven Brides* series, which is set in a fashionable English spa town frequented by the great and the bad of Regency society.

Connect with Mary on-line – she loves to hear from readers:

Email Mary:
Mary@MaryLancaster.com

Website:
www.MaryLancaster.com

Newsletter sign-up:
http://eepurl.com/b4Xoif

Facebook:
facebook.com/mary.lancaster.1656

Facebook Author Page:
facebook.com/MaryLancasterNovelist

Twitter:
@MaryLancNovels

Amazon Author Page:
amazon.com/Mary-Lancaster/e/B00DJ5IACI

Bookbub:
bookbub.com/profile/mary-lancaster